Combination Lock

and Other Stories

Patrick Vaughn

P+6 -
you guys are
the best.
Patrick Vaughn

For my Misty, without whose love there could be no dreams.

Contents

Preface   vii

Combination Lock   1

An Act of Mercy   62

Hope & Dez   94

An Easy Target   99

The DanneR Party   132

Preface

I LIKE TO WRITE. I ALWAYS HAVE, WHETHER IT'S A NOVEL, an e-mail, a journal/blog entry, even a facebook status. And sometimes my stories come out in mixed media, as I find the different perspectives interesting and fun to play with.

Combination Lock is my best example of mixing media — it contains journal entries, chat transcripts, e-mails, even a newspaper article. And I initially released the story as a serial via e-mail, so that time could be another factor. My readers - a dozen or so people on an email list service - would literally have to wait the same time periods that took place in the story before reading what happened next. It was a lot of fun to write and to share.

An Act of Mercy was released serially but really didn't need to be. It's more of a straight-ahead short story that bounces back and forth through time. I include it here because it's my favorite of my shorter works.

Hope and Dez is my version of a short short story. When I was a teenager I received a short short story compilation as a gift, and so, for about the next year, every story I wrote fit on two pages of text. This is the best one of the bunch; the rest read a bit like watching a television show in fast-forward.

An Easy Target is my latest short work, where I tell a story with minimal narrative: the bulk of the story takes place in interviews, diary entries and medical reports. It wasn't easy to write, but the words flew out of me because I was having so much fun.

Finally, **The DanneR Party** is the transcription of a blog that I wrote online leading up to the release of my first novel, The Cure for the Curse. It takes place right before page 1 of the novel, and again I was able to release the entries in time with the story, so if two days passed in the story, two days would pass before another entry was available. The blog is still available online - you can get to it from patrickvaughn.net - and I definitely recommend seeing it in the online incarnation, as there's fun things I could do with links that just don't come across on the written page. But I wanted to preserve it in print, and so it rounds out this collection.

A word of caution: all of these stories deal with material that's far more intense than my young adult novels. I would strongly advise all the parents out there to read the stories before sharing them with anyone younger than 16... or else be prepared to answer some unpleasant questions.

Enjoy!

-Patrick Vaughn
February 2012

Combination Lock

August 19, 2008

This is a bad idea.

But Dr. P would say to write it out, so I can take possession of it. Whatever that means. So here goes.

I had a strange dream last night. I was in a dim hallway, and I found a book on a dirty tile floor. The book had a blank cover, and when I opened it up I get hit with this bright flash of light.

Then I'm wide awake in my bed, covered in cold sweat. And I've got this number burning a hole in my head:

156761293X33710937434848479712216142

I had to write it down, had to get it out of me. It's weird, I woke up exactly like I was having a nightmare from the bad times, but the only feeling I had this morning was a fear that I would lose that number. I couldn't get back to sleep, so I figured I'd put it in my journal too. But that hasn't helped. I still feel twitchy, like I just drank two pots of coffee. Looks like I go to work on 3 hours of sleep.

I've never remembered a number from a dream before. Oh well, it's in my journal now. I've got possession of it.

Whatever that means.

\<rachelp\>	hey
\<EIN1104\>	hey yourself
\<EIN1104\>	What are you doing up? I never see you online this late.
\<EIN1104\>	Isn't it like 3 in the morning for you?
\<rachelp\>	can't sleep. weird dream
\<EIN1104\>	do tell
\<rachelp\>	don't remember much. looked in a book, woke up. now I've got this number stuck in my head
\<EIN1104\>	A number? Like a tune, or like a phone #?
\<rachelp\>	number as in the things you count with. it's too long to be a phone #
\<rachelp\>	156761293X33710937434847 9712216142
\<rachelp\>	I'm wide awake & that number is all I can remember
\<EIN1104\>	That's really strange, Rache.
\<rachelp\>	tell me about it
\<EIN1104\>	No, really. I've read about this.
\<EIN1104\>	Dreaming takes place away from the language centers of the brain.
\<EIN1104\>	That's why it's so hard to read a book or newspaper in a dream.
\<rachelp\>	so?
\<EIN1104\>	So, dreaming happens even farther away from any logic center that could perceive or retain something as complex as a 34-digit number.
\<EIN1104\>	Heck, I have trouble remembering my own phone number, and that's only 10 digits!
\<rachelp\>	well it's there. and it had to come from someplace
\<EIN1104\>	Maybe an alien was whispering that # in your ear while you slept.
\<rachelp\>	when it could have been probing me?
\<rachelp\>	I've been cheated

August 20, 2008

This recording my thoughts stuff was fun this morning. Maybe there's something behind this "take possession of it" thing. It's like I have someone to talk to that I know won't forget what I've said.

I went to my nightshift at K-Mart feeling a little foggy, still thinking about that dream. Nobody bugged me though. I really like that about this job. I can go for hours without having to talk to anybody. Plus I get to clean as many floors as I want.

Anyway, I was staring at the DVD rack, just sorta spacing out, when one of the Mexican girls says "They all look so happy, don't they." She was pointing at the rack of musicals I'd been looking at, and we got to talking. She likes "Seven Brides for Seven Brothers" because they all end up one enormous happy family.

Everything works out for everybody in those old movies. All the problems are just misunderstandings because everybody's healthy and basically good at heart. There's no trauma to recover from, no Demoral to get addicted to, no doctors that touch your ass. Not that I said any of that.

Anyway, that girl's name is Ynes, said like "ee-NESS". Before today she was just another of the Mexican girls who rolled their eyes at me and talked in Spanish behind my back. But now she's Ynes. And I managed to not say anything stupid to someone being nice to me. Well, I probably didn't.

I'm having a hard time forgetting about that dream, though. Maybe having a different one will do the trick.

August 21, 2008

It didn't do the trick.

I don't think I dreamt anything, I just watched that long number bob up and down in my head, like a roller-coaster of digits plummeting and coasting behind my eyes. Oh well, sleep has always been a fleeting thing for me. It's bound to come back sooner or later.

I had today off, so I visited mom. I brought her the darkest red tulip I could find at the flower shop, and gave her stone a good wipe-down. It was a cloudy, quiet day, and I had a long talk with her. She's proud that I've stayed out of the hospital on my own for so long, but she's worried that I don't have enough friends. I told mom that I have lots of friends online, but she wasn't buying. And honestly, neither was I. My online 'friends' live in a glowing box that I can turn on and off at will. People don't really exist if they can't touch you. I guess that makes them more like ghosts.

Then I told her about Ynes, who isn't a friend really, but she was nice to me. Mom said I should be nice back to her. It's the decent thing to do.

I hope I can get some sleep tonight. I want to be awake if someone is nice to me again.

August 22, 2008

Still not much sleeping, just thinking about that stupid number. I can recite it from memory now. It's like a song stuck in my head, but with numbers instead of notes.

Ynes was nice to me again today. We talked about Johnny Depp and how we both would sign up for harem duty, no questions asked. We giggled. I can't remember the last time I giggled with someone.

Ynes has a really big smile, and she opens her mouth wide when she laughs. I hardly ever open my mouth at all for any reason.

She asked me if I wanted to get a cup of coffee after work. My old reflex kicked in and I said 'no thanks,' but when I saw her frowning I said how about tomorrow?

I'm really nervous. I'm worried she'll figure out how messed up I am.

I know I'm a lot better than I used to be. I'm independent, out on my own, paying my own bills. I don't have those dark thoughts anymore, and the memories are locked away in a place where they can't hurt anybody. Yeah, I'm a lot better, I know that. And mom knows that too. But I'd rather Ynes didn't know how messed up I was. I doubt she'd want to have coffee with somebody with the potential to do the things I did. I know I wouldn't.

Sleep would be a nice thing.

<rachelp>	hey eric
<EIN1104>	Yah Rache, how r u?
<rachelp>	good
<rachelp>	can I ask you something
<EIN1104>	Sure
<rachelp>	my phone
<rachelp>	keeps ringing
<EIN1104>	Well, you could stop paying your phone bill...
<rachelp>	like once and whoever it is has hung up by the time I answer
<rachelp>	sorry am typing lefthanded
<EIN1104>	That's OK
<EIN1104>	Have you tried *69?
<rachelp>	yah
<rachelp>	I get a function not available msg
<EIN1104>	Which means your caller dialed *70 before dialing.
<EIN1104>	You have caller ID?
<rachelp>	yah
<rachelp>	sez unavailable
<EIN1104>	Well... if this caller is harassing you, you could get the police to get the phone company's log of calls.
<rachelp>	uh huh
<EIN1104>	How many times has this happened?
<rachelp>	3
<rachelp>	over the past four days or so
<EIN1104>	Well if it keeps up, the cops might help you,
<EIN1104>	but for now I think you're on your own.
<rachelp>	that's ok
<rachelp>	I'm online all the time anyway
<EIN1104>	Hey Rachel, how come you're typing lefthanded?
<rachelp>	um

<rachelp>	my right hand is busy
<EIN1104>	Kinky!
<EIN1104>	I didn't know you practiced the ol' Type n Tickle ;)
<rachelp>	not what you think
<rachelp>	it's much weirder

August 23, 2008

I ended up writing the number out in pen on notebook paper until I got tired enough to sleep for a few hours. I filled up seven pages, front and back. I did it while chatting online, though. That makes it less crazy, right?

I managed to keep it together for coffee with Ynes after work. Well, mostly.

Turns out we've both lived in Mesa all our lives and actually live in the same part of town. She said I remind her of her quiet little sister, who she calls Lencia, which is like an abbreviated way to say 'silent' in Spanish. We talked about work, mostly. She told me that all the Mexican girls actually like working with me because I'll do the floors. They say the soap burns their skin. I've never minded the stinging. As long as I can get the floors clean, I don't care if it hurts.

I sort of lost it when she asked about the streaks in my hair. She wanted to know how I get them to my particular shade of red, so I told her about the dye I use, and how I found the tube in mom's bathroom. . . and before I knew it my tears were dripping off my chin. It's so hard to keep track of all the conversation topics that can lead to those bad places. All paths seem to lead down the mountain. It's so much easier to not say anything. If you never take any first steps, you never go down.

Ynes was nice about it, though. She said she recognized the look in my eyes, because Lencia had it too. How'd she say it? Like my eyes 'overflowed from seeing too much too soon.' I didn't ask if Lencia still had that look. But I get the feeling Lencia's gone. Whenever Ynes says her sister's name, the corners of her mouth dip for a second. I think something happened, but I'm not about to pry.

Ynes is a sweetheart. I'm going to make her some of mom's peanut butter cookies.

. . .I just discovered that the more I write out the number, the easier it is to concentrate. I was just making a shopping list, and I wrote the number out in between each of the items. I'm pretty sure Dr. P would call this obsessive, but it can't be all bad. I managed to make a friend while undergoing all this. At least I hope I did.

August 24, 2008

The cookies turned out okay after the first batch, which was way too salty. But this headache makes it really hard to think.

I've tried Tylenol, Advil and caffeine, but nothing's getting rid of it. It does feel better when I'm writing the number out, though. And even better when I say it out loud. Probably not good.

Ynes thanked me for the cookies. Some of the other Mexican girls – Rosa, Hiris and Celia – saw me give them to her and giggled. They said something in Spanish and Ynes laughed.

She told me they asked when we – Ynes and me – were getting married, and were we registered there at K-Mart?

My face got really hot.

Ynes told them it would take a lot more than cookies to get her off of men. But then she saw my reaction. After the other girls left she asked me if I was gay. She was concerned, not angry. I told her I wasn't gay, and that I thought maybe there was some Mexican cookie-giving custom that I was oblivious to, that it meant something obvious and important, because that'd be the sort of thing that everybody knows, and I only manage to find out while embarrassing myself. She smiled that big smile and told me there wasn't any cookie-giving custom that she knew about, and that it was okay if I was gay, but I should know that she isn't.

I assured her that I'm not gay. And I know I'm not. I'm not straight, either. I'm nothing. It's the safest thing to be.

I'm glad Ynes didn't ask me to go anywhere after work with her. My headache was pretty bad since I couldn't say the number at work. And I'd never be able to recite it in front of her.

I hope the headache goes away.

August 25, 2008

The headache is worse. The pain is a steady pounding on the left side of my head, but the throbbing doesn't match my heartbeat. It's a lot faster... unless I'm writing out or saying that stupid number from that stupid dream I had LAST WEEK!

What could this stupid number mean, anyway?

156761293X33710937434848479712216142

I mean, it's 34 digits, for shit's sake. I entered it into google, but all I got were errors. It's probably a serial number from an aircraft part or something else totally random and meaningless. And what's with that X? It sticks out like the birthmark on my ear. But I know it belongs there. That's its home, just between the first and second 3's.

Ugh. I know I shouldn't obsess on it. There's probably no real connection between my headache and the number. I'm probably just losing it again. But I didn't do anything this time! I've kept the dark thoughts away!

I should call Dr. P. But what if she sends me to the hospital? I'll have to start all over again, more pills, more therapy sessions. All the work of the last three years undone. By what? A number that came to me in a dream??

No!

I can do this. I can beat this. I just have to get it out of me, that's all. Yeah. The number is stuck in my brain, which is making it ache. I have to get it out. I can do that. I'm stronger than any number.

August 26, 2008

The headache is better today. But I'm not sure it's worth it.

I used up all my notebook paper pretty quickly. But around 2pm I had a good idea: the margins of the phone book! Lots of pages there. But my hand started to cramp up. The pain wasn't as bad as the headache, but I couldn't get the muscles to work. So, I used a marker, and I noticed that the larger I drew the numbers, the better my head felt.

I drew one number per phonebook page. I needed to see the complete number together – if I turned the page the pain came back. So I ripped out each page and taped it to the wall.

My apartment is a Vanna White nightmare. All over the walls are yellow pages with giant black numbers on them. I made sure there's full number in each room, wrapping around the walls. When I look at them the ache gets better. I used lipstick to draw it on the bathroom mirror, and it's even on the ceiling of my bedroom. I'm sure it's what let me sleep last night.

I thought about my floor. What if my downstairs neighbors could look through it and see my room and all those numbers? Ha! They'd have me put me away in a second.

The dark thoughts are coming. I can feel them, like when the air feels heavier before the rain.

The most frustrating part about all this is that I didn't do anything to start it. It's not like I made a bad choice, or that I did one of Dr. P's 'chaos-acts.' I just had a dream. I can't stop those.

It's like some dark piece of me wants me to end up mumbling in an alley with a shopping cart full of smelly rags. And I can't do anything to stop her. All I can do is try to stay out of her way.

Well, maybe somebody else can stop her. I'm calling Dr. P tomorrow. I owe that much to Mom.

But I can't help but feel like I'm starting all over again.

\<EIN1104\>	Hi Rache
\<rachelp\>	hi eric
\<EIN1104\>	your phone still doing that thing?
\<rachelp\>	not since last week
\<EIN1104\>	that's good
\<EIN1104\>	what's up today?
\<rachelp\>	just wondering if you exist or not
\<EIN1104\>	Well, here I am.
\<rachelp\>	you could be a computer program for all I know
\<EIN1104\>	NEED MORE INPUT TO ANSWER QUESTION
\<rachelp\>	ha
\<EIN1104\>	What, am I that predictable?
\<rachelp\>	no... I don't mean that
\<rachelp\>	I mean how do I *really* know that you exist?
\<EIN1104\>	You mean how do you know I'm not some middle-aged software designer with raging halitosis and craterous backne pretending to be a semi-studly soph at Cal Sacramento with a killer ping-pong forehand?
\<rachelp\>	sorta
\<rachelp\>	I guess how do I know you're not a fabrication of my own brain?
\<rachelp\>	a psychosis in the form of glowing black letters on my screen?
\<EIN1104\>	Ah, the old 'how do I know reality is real' question.
\<EIN1104\>	I think the answer to that question – and how you know I'm not Artie Schmidlap with bad breath & backne come back to the same thing.
\<rachelp\>	and that is?
\<EIN1104\>	Trust. You have to trust that I'm who I say I am.
\<EIN1104\>	And you have to trust yourself.
\<EIN1104\>	That your senses aren't deceiving you.

\<rachelp\>	!! That's funny!
\<EIN1104\>	?
\<rachelp\>	no, eric it's a good point. a great point.
\<rachelp\>	but every shrink I've ever seen has told me I have trust issues

---

August 27, 2008

I called in sick to work, and Dr. P was nice enough to see me today. She's puzzled by the suddenness of the obsession. She thinks that I'm reacting to forming a bond with an actual person (Ynes). This obsession is an excuse to push her away, and go back to the safety of my solitude.

I don't know about that. I had the dream before Ynes was nice to me. Dr. P also says the number doesn't have any meaning, other than the headache it produces and how thinking about it distracts me from doing healthy things. But I can't escape the feeling that the number is a key to a door somewhere. A door I'll never find.

But she's the doctor. She helped me stay out of the hospital this long. And she's never once tried to touch me.

She started me on a new medication. It makes me sleepy, but the headache is already much better. It's not gone, but it's more of an itch now. Or maybe a tickle.

I still feel different when I write out the number. It's like the Superstition Mountains. I can gauge where I am in the city as long as I can see those mountains. And I get that same feeling when I write out that number. Like I know my place.

I've taken down all those yellow pages with the black numbers so my apartment doesn't look like a psychopath's den anymore. But I'm leaving the pages on my bedroom ceiling. Just in case.

August 28, 2008

I went back to work today. It felt good to clean some floors again. But the new medicine makes me think slower, and I embarrassed myself in front of Ynes.

I was filling out my time sheet, and as I stopped to add up the hours, Ynes asked me what I was writing in the margins. I'd written the number three times without realizing it, and was ten digits into writing it again. I told Ynes that I didn't know, that it was nothing, but I stuttered so bad I knew she could tell I was lying.

Then she said the number looked like an ISBN. When I asked her what that was, she said it's the number on the backs of the paperbacks over by the greeting cards. She said she picks one book every couple of weeks to read during her lunch break. It helps her learn English.

When I asked her which books she reads, she blushed. I didn't know Mexican girls *could* blush. Anyway, she pointed to her chest and said 'the ones that get my heart beating.'

I made her promise not to tell anyone about my number. She said she wouldn't as long as I didn't tell anybody about her romance novels. So we both have a secret. At least hers is normal.

What she said about the number stuck with me. I've thought of it as one complete thing, but maybe it has parts? But how do I know how many parts? And where to divide it?

I probably shouldn't think about it. This is how people go crazy: searching for life-altering meaning in something totally random.

It's time for my next pill. So that means it's time for bed.

August 29, 2008

I think I found something. Or maybe something found me.

This morning I was thinking about the number – what else? – and then I remembered the dream that started all this. The number came to me when I opened a *book*.

So I went to amazon.com and entered the first ten digits of the number. And it's the ISBN of a book:

"Moonpulse," by Richard Anthony Persson.

It was published a couple of years ago by a place I've never heard of, "Fantastic Planet Press." Apparently it's a werewolf story; there weren't any reviews on the page, just a blurb on the plot designed to hook a potential reader.

I've never liked horror stories, and the name "Richard Anthony Persson" doesn't mean anything to me... but that itch in my head became a hum as soon as I saw that title.

There's something important about this book. I can feel it. But amazon says it'll be a week before they can ship it. I checked a couple of other online book stores, and they were even slower.

I've placed an order, and paid for overnight shipping. But I'm going to go check the library, and all the bookstores around town. I have to have this book. I don't really know what I'm expecting to find. But I know there's something inside it especially for me. There has to be. The hum is evidence enough of that.

I'm definitely not going to tell Dr. P about this. She'll just say it's another stage of the obsession. And so what if it is? All I'm out so far is $19.95.

I have to go, I want to check a couple of stores before going to work. I thought about calling in sick again, but I really need to scrub some floors tonight.

August 30, 2008

No luck finding 'Moonpulse.' A nice clerk at Waldenbooks explained why. Apparently 'Fantastic Planet Press' is a publish-on-demand place, which basically means when somebody wants a copy of the book, they print one. They don't just keep piles of them around at bookstores.

The clerk told me they could order a copy, but it'd be at least two weeks before it came in, and that was going to be the case at any bookstore.

So it looks like I have another six days to wait. But the hum in my head is constant. It's a low, rushing sound, like water moving through pipes in the wall across the room. I even hear it when I'm outside.

But it's a lot better than the headache. And the number eases it a little.

I'm getting sleepy.

<rachelp>	hi mal
<malFina>	hello rachel
<malFina>	what you up to
<rachelp>	106 lbs
<rachelp>	this new medicine has done wonders for my appetite
<rachelp>	I'm shoveling in the french fries
<malFina>	you're evil, you know that?
<rachelp>	yeah, I know
<malFina>	I think I hate my neighbor
<rachelp>	the girl or the old man?
<malFina>	the girl
<malFina>	she jogs by my balcony every night
<malFina>	with her cute little sweat shorts
<malFina>	and her perfect little ponytail
<malFina>	I hate her
<rachelp>	yeah?
<rachelp>	does she roll her eyes at you or something?
<malFina>	no... she always smiles at me
<malFina>	she's just so damn perfect
<rachelp>	yeah, how dare she be all healthy like that
<rachelp>	where does she get off
<malFina>	:P
<malFina>	you're evil, you know that?
<rachelp>	yeah, I know

September 1, 2008

Not much to report. Had the day off, which seemed to take forever, cuz I know there's four more after it that I'll have to wait to get my book. I poked around the "Fantastic Planet Press" website, and found this bio about Richard Anthony Persson:

"Mr. Persson has been writing weird tales since he was a boy, when an old 'Wolfman' movie sparked his interest in the darker side of the human psyche. 'Moonpulse' is his first full-length novel, but he has an archive of flash fiction and poetry at www.geocities.com/users/lycanden.html. He lives in the Sierra Nevadas, where he communes with the Mother and howls at the moon."

The link is broken, of course. Doesn't say much about the guy himself, does it? I did a google search, but I don't have much to go on to figure out which "Richard Persson" is the same one that wrote this book. Those "Wolfman" movies have been around since at least the sixties... and it doesn't say when he moved to the Sierra Nevadas, just that he now lives there. And it could be a penname...

I was really bored today. I wanted to do some reading, but I couldn't keep my attention on the page. I think it's probably the drugs. I ended up chatting online while watching TV... for around six hours. There's a dark thought banging on the door, but I'm not going to let it in. One day of boredom doesn't represent my whole life.

Right?

September 2, 2008

Wow, what a day. Ynes asked me if I wanted to catch a movie with her after work. I told her that the theatres don't have morning shows, but she meant a tape at her place. I immediately said no, but she wasn't having any of it. She'd rented Benny & Joon, and I was going to watch it on her couch this morning. That was that.

So I did!

Ynes lives in a tiny apartment that she shares with a girl named Lupe, who was leaving for her job just as we arrived. Ynes showed me her bedroom. She has a couple of amazing velvet paintings of what's probably the Virgin mother... and a Don Juan DeMarco movie poster on her ceiling. (Way more normal than what's currently on MY bedroom ceiling.)

Anyway, we watched the movie and ate microwave popcorn. Every now and then Ynes would hit pause, apologize for doing so, then ask me what a word meant. Like 'revelation,' or 'fraudulent.' I'd explain the meaning, she'd smile, pronounce the word one more time, say thank you, then push play.

It's a pretty old movie, but it's still good. I was crying at the end, when Benny and Joon are finally together. I was happy for them, but I was sad too. I'll never find any Benny. He's just a movie character played by a gorgeous actor in a work of fiction. Crazy girls don't get Johnny Depp. We get guys like Derek, and Dr. McCarty. Guys who just want sex and don't think twice about lying to you about anything.

I was glad I went to Ynes's place, though. It made me feel normal, and I didn't notice the humming sound till the drive home.

Three more days till 'Moonpulse' comes. I see Dr. P tomorrow, but I'm not going to mention the book. What she doesn't know won't hurt her.

September 3, 2008

Saw Dr. P today. She's really happy about the movie-night/morning with Ynes yesterday. Says I've made great progress. The headaches being gone are good too, but she's more impressed by the developing friendship.

I guess I am too. But there's so much about my past that I can't share. I don't want Ynes to think I'm a freak, but friends tell each other about themselves. Maybe I'll make something up… like I've spent the last five years recovering from cancer. Or maybe I've got amnesia. Or survived a plane crash.

Nah. I can't back anything like that up.

Speaking of making stuff up, I told Dr. P that I hadn't thought about the number since I went on the new drug. It's sort of true. I don't write it out anymore. But I didn't say anything about the humming, and how anxious I am to read 'Moonpulse.' And those black numbers are still stuck to my bedroom ceiling…

But I feel pretty good, overall, and Dr. P could tell. And that's all that really matters.

Two more days 'til my book comes.

<malFina>	this boy was flirting with me in Walgreens today
<rachelp>	oh yeah?
<rachelp>	you tell him you prefer girls?
<malFina>	no
<malFina>	he was really cute. probably the cutest guy I've ever seen
<malFina>	my heart melted like ice cream in the summer sun
<rachelp>	!
<malFina>	did I mention he was 2 yrs old
<rachelp>	very funny :P
<malFina>	seriously though. he was CUTE! big brown eyes, smooth black hair, and he wasn't terrorizing the store or his parents. got me feeling things.
<rachelp>	clock ticking?
<malFina>	maybe...
<malFina>	even though I know it's just nature, it doesn't change how friggin' cute that boy was
<rachelp>	yeah, but he's gonna grow up to be a man
<rachelp>	and get ugly in all those places
<malFina>	maybe he will, maybe he won't
<malFina>	you ever feel the urge? the baby bug?
<rachelp>	nope
<rachelp>	I've got bad mothering genes
<rachelp>	trust me on this one
<malFina>	but you've never once felt that desire?
<malFina>	that ache in your heart when you see some cute kidlet?
<rachelp>	well
<malFina>	mmm?
<rachelp>	every once in a while I want one just because it's what normal people do

<rachelp>	they have kids, fuck them up, so the kids grow up fucked up, then those kids raise kids of their own that they unintentionally fuck up, those kids grow up fucked up, etc.
<rachelp>	it's the circle of life
<rachelp>	I should play my part
<malFina>	geez
<malFina>	get your tubes tied NOW!
<rachelp>	ha
<malFina>	what do you want to be normal for?
<rachelp>	normal people have normal problems. normal sounds easy
<malFina>	yeah, but then you'd have to be normal
<rachelp>	'normal' would be a significant improvement for me
<rachelp>	hang on, someone's knocking
<malFina>	fuck normal. normal is boring.
<malFina>	k
<malFina>	Rachel?
<malFina>	hello?

September 4, 2008

It came!
Amazon didn't freaking email me that it was coming, but my book came today! I've read it twice already. It's kind of long, and there are a couple of parts that don't make any sense. But the humming is GONE when I'm reading it.

However…

There's nothing in it that really stands out. I don't get it. I was certain there was something very important in this book for me – that the number had pointed me to it. But it's just a story about a guy who's a werewolf, who finds out he's actually the result of some government conspiracy experiment (or experimental conspiracy, I'm not really sure.) I couldn't identify with the main character at all... well, except when they put him in the nuthouse.

Ugh. As I've typed this, the humming has returned and become really loud. But if I stick my nose in the pages it shuts off. My brain wants me to read this book. But why? What's in there that I'm missing? Or am I just trying to go insane?

No, that's a dark thought. And I can't let them in.

September 5, 2008

Pain is awful. Headache, like spiked ball bouncing inside my head, shredding brain with every heartbeat. Better only when speaking number while reading book.

Called sick to work. Dr. P can't see me til tomorrow. Said I should go to hospital if pain is unbearable. Can't go to hospital. Never go to hospital again. Rather die.

Book has nothing for me. No significance on any page. Same with my life.

Dark thoughts surround. Defenses are down. Don't know how I'll make it through the day.

Can't give up. Owe it to mom.

September 6, 2008

It was the number all along. The rest of the digits are a map.

The headache is gone, and it feels like I'm buzzing on caffeine. I've never been more awake in my life. My eyes are wide open, and my heart is beating gently but quickly. But I've reached another crossroad.

I'll explain:

337109374348479712216142 are the rest of the digits after the ISBN.

I treated them like they were referring to chapter and verse. Like in the bible. So, the first few digits after the X are

33710

That ended up meaning page 33, line 7, word 10. It took some time to figure out where the dividers came, but I caught on pretty quick. That first word: wolf. Big surprise.

9374

page 93, line 7, word 4: den

3484

page 34, line 8, word 4: at

797

page 7, line 9, word 7: moonlight

1221

page 12, line 2, word 1: dot   (from "make sure you/dot all the i's and cross all the t's")

6142

page 6, line 14, word 2: net   ("it was like walking a tightrope without/a net...")

Yup. It's a goddamn email address:

wolfden@moonlight.net

That's what the dream, the number, the headaches, the humming have led to. I'm sure of it. I did a google search and found that address used on a message board on a fansite of some Japanese cartoon that of course has werewolves as a major theme. The writer didn't have many posts, but he or she used the phrase 'heaping pile of dirty dogshit' in one of them, a phrase that's used twice in 'Moonpulse.'

It has to be Richard Persson. But now what? I've got to write to him, but what do I say? 'Hi, your email address popped out of my head. What's up?'

I've got to get to work. I can't miss any more days, and I think scrubbing some floors will help me come up with what to write.

And I cancelled my appointment with Dr. P. I told her I just mismanaged the dose on my drug and that I feel fine now. I think she bought it.

Date: Tue, 7 Sep 2008 07:22:17 -0700
From: rachelP@dystopia.net
To: wolfden@moonlight.net
Sub: are you who I think you are?
Parts/Attachments: None

Hi,

I saw you post as waxwane04 on the Howler forum, and I have to ask:
Did you write a book called "Moonpulse", published by Fantastic Planet Press in 2002, ISBN 1-56761-293-X?
If you are Richard Anthony Persson, I'd really like to talk to you about your book. It really affected me, and I'd like to ask about your inspirations, motivations & such.
If you're not R.A.P., then I apologize for wasting your time, but please let me know as much so I can look somewhere else.

See you on the forums,
Rachel

September 7, 2008

I'm exhausted.

I was really spacey at work as I thought about what to put in my letter to The Email Address That Sprang From Inside My Brain (or TEATSFIMB). I ended up playing it pretty close to the vest. It was the only choice, really. Anything more would scare him away. If it's even him.

I screwed up and told Ynes – who was concerned at the sick days I'd been taking, she's such a sweetie – the same story I gave Dr. P. That I'd mismanaged my medication, which had given me a killer headache. She didn't ask what I was taking the drug for. She did ask if I wanted to go to a park with her after work. I told her there was something important I had to do. She didn't ask me what that thing was, but she did ask if it would take me very long. I said no because I couldn't come up with anything else.

So, I came home and wrote the email. I agonized over it for a while, but the fact that Ynes was waiting for me sped up the process.

Actually she was just feeding the geese in this pond at a golf course. And that's all she wanted to do. It was really nice. The morning was cloudy, and very cool, like the last time I visited mom. She mentioned that Lencia had liked feeding the ducks at Saguaro Lake. She said Lencia always looked at peace while she threw the bread crusts, and she hoped Lencia was near a pond with lots of ducks. I don't know if that meant that Lencia died, or lives far away now. I didn't ask, but I said "it sounds like you miss her a lot." She nodded. She said she misses Lencia the most at night, so that's why she works night shifts. So the stars won't remind her of her little sister.

It kinda sucked that I was all excited about my email to TEATSFIMB but I couldn't share any of it with Ynes. But I'm never going to tell her about it. That would be a chaos-act: I know it would frighten her away, so I'm not going to do it. No matter how much I want to.

I need to get some sleep. It's been a long day.

**rachelp80 has entered channel #somniloquy

**Topic for channel #somniloquy: "No one is completely unhappy at the failure of his best friend" – Groucho Marx

<reetah>   which isn't at all what I meant

<CoEsthar>   hey rachel

<leastdef>   hi rache

<Al/Killa>   sup r8

<rachelp80> hi everyone

<reetah>   he was only hearing what he wanted to

<Anaranjad> well, you've always known – or at least suspected – that he was really self-centered at heart

<rachelp80> got a question for the group

<Al/Killa>   OK

<leastdef>   shoot

<CoEsthar>   I'm listening

<rachelp80> ok

<reetah>   I knew he could get like that

<rachelp80> anybody here ever hear of a show called "Howler?"

<rachelp80> (it's animated)

<reetah>   But I never thought he *was* like that

<leastdef>   nope

<Anaranjad> hi Rachel, and no

<Al/Killa>   doesn't ring any bells, r8

<CoEsthar>   hmmm

<Anaranjad> rita – so are you two broken up?

<rachelp80> crap

<reetah>   no

```
<reetah>      I haven't decided if I'm going to
              or not
<CoEsthar>    wait a min, Rachel
<reetah>      break up with him, I mean
<rachelp80>   got something, CoE?
<Al/Killa>    what a waffler
<CoEsthar>    yeah
<CoEsthar>    I remember now
*reetah has changed her name to waffleiron
<CoEsthar>    I saw a few eps of an anime called
              "The Howlers of Tsinijira"
*waffleiron irons some waffles
<Anaranjad>   ha
<rachelp80>   that's prolly it
*leastdef wants some waffles
<rachelp80>   what u think of it?
<Al/Killa>    who *doesn't* want a piece of
              waffle? *wink*
<CoEsthar>    started with interesting idea,
              then got real weird
*waffleiron has PLENTY to go around
<rachelp80> can you describe it for me?
<CoEsthar> sure
*Anaranjad prefers flapjacks
*rachelp80 has left channel #somniloquy
<CoEsthar> there's these kids — mostly
           teenagers, some a little older
<CoEsthar> and they're werewolves, but
           they're on some drug that keeps
           them from transforming
<CoEsthar> and they're trying to live semi-
           normal lives
```

<CoEsthar> while trying to find other werewolves who aren't yet on the drug

<CoEsthar> (and not get ripped to shreds by same)

<CoEsthar> but it turns out the company that makes the drug that keeps them human is actually spreading the condition

<CoEsthar> making more werewolves, so more people have to have the drug, which means more money

<rachelp80> huh

<CoEsthar> then it started getting into demons, and "original werewolves" and shit

<CoEsthar> it got to be less about the characters dealing with the affliction

<CoEsthar> and more about the hierarchy of demons and how they're in modern corporations or something

<CoEsthar> it sucked

<rachelp80> do you know how it ends?

<CoEsthar> no, sorry

<CoEsthar> I didn't know you were into anime

<rachelp80> I'm not

<rachelp80> but somebody I know is

Date: Wed, 8 Sep 2008 22:55:18 -0800
From: wolfden@moonlight.net
To: rachelP@dystopia.net
Sub: re: are you who I think you are?
Parts/Attachments: None

Dear Rachel,

Wow. Yes, I wrote "Moonpulse" under the name Richard
Anthony Persson and published it with Fantastic Planet Press
in '04. I'll be happy to answer any questions you have as long
as you tell me one thing:
How did you find me? "Moonpulse" sold about 31 copies, all
either bought by me or by people I personally browbeat into
buying it. Do I know you? Are you a friend of a friend?
I'm sorry if I seem confrontational, but I've been hounded by
scammers ever since I started trying to get "Moonpulse"
published, and I'd like to make certain you're not one before
going any further.

Sincerely,
Tony K.

Date: Thurs, 9 Sep 2008 07:33:47 -0700
From: rachelP@dystopia.net
To: wolfden@moonlight.net
Sub: Moonpulse
Parts/Attachments: None

Tony,

I promise I'm not a scam. I'm not out to sell you anything. I just want to talk about your book.
I guessed it was you from the phrase 'heaping pile of dirty dogs---' that you used on the Howler forum. I picked up your book a few months back as an impulse buy – I was on the FPP site looking up a friend's title, where I read your blurb. "Moonpulse" looked interesting, so I bought it.
I truly can't get enough of it. Can you tell me what inspired you to write it? My favorite scene is the one in the sanitarium, where Ivan starts to believe all the doctors that tell him he's crazy. Is there any particular motivation for that scene?
I'm sorry if I'm being annoying. It just seems very lucky that I found you, and I want to take advantage of the opportunity.

Thanks,
R.

Date: Fri, 10 Sep 2008 23:03:55 -0800
From: wolfden@moonlight.net
To: rachelP@dystopia.net
Sub: yeah, uh-huh
Parts/Attachments: None

Rachel,

I'm not really sure where the idea for "Moonpulse" came
from. It probably came to me while watching an episode of X-
Files or reading Fantasy & Sci-Fi Magazine. As for the scene
with Ivan at St. Luke's, I remember seeing the steeple of a
church when I was visiting a friend in Tucson, Arizona. He
told me that property was actually a mental hospital, and that
seemed like a great idea for the setting of a sanitarium.
But I don't believe your story. You're saying that not only did
you browse at a P-O-D website – which nobody does, nor has
reason to – but you also happened to be part of a forum for an
obscure anime that has never been dubbed into a western
language and isn't for sale anywhere outside of Japan. That's
too much coincidence for me to swallow.
I will not continue this correspondence any further until you
tell me the truth.
And I'll save us both some time: I'm not interested in any
'promotional kit' for "Moonpulse." If it didn't sell another
copy that'd be fine with me.

Tony

September 11, 2008

'Tony', the author of "Moonpulse" and the owner of TEATSFIMB, isn't being very helpful. He seems pretty paranoid, which I probably could've guessed from reading his book, what with all the layers of conspiracy going on in it. Or probably going on in it. I've read it twelve times so far, and I'm still not sure what's really happening to the character, as opposed to what he just *thinks* is happening.

Anyway, I don't know what I want Tony to say. Each time I read his emails I buzz like the night I figured out the number code: eyes wide open, heart racing, fingers twitching. I've combed his words for meaning, but the only thing that seems familiar is that hospital in Tucson.

I know I did some time in Tucson on two different occasions. But I don't remember any church steeple. But then, there's a lot of that time locked away inside me that I don't ever want to remember again. And I was pretty doped up for a lot of it too.

I feel like if I could just get Tony to be honest with me, he might reveal something important. But I don't know how I'm going to break through the paranoia.

With time, I guess. The layers of fear will peel away as I continue to write him without asking for anything.

Well, anything but words.

Date: Sat, 11 Sep 2008 09:22:02 -0700
From: rachelP@dystopia.net
To: wolfden@moonlight.net
Sub: re: yeah, uh-huh
Parts/Attachments: None

Tony,

I promise you, my intentions are pure! I don't want your money, I just want some insight into your book.
I'll admit I didn't browse the Fantastic Planet website. The truth is, I obtained a copy of your book in sort of a semi-embarrassing way that I'd rather not talk about. But does it really matter how I got it? I want to know more about it, and you.
Don't sell yourself short, Tony. This book has CAPTIVATED me. I don't know what else I can say to assure you that I'm not out to scam you.

Please believe me,

Rachel

Date: Sat, 11 Sep 2008 18:27:48 -0800
From: wolfden@moonlight.net
To: rachelP@dystopia.net
Sub: no dice
Parts/Attachments: None

Rachel,

> Don't sell yourself short, Tony. This book has
> CAPTIVATED me. I don't know what else I can say to
> assure you that I'm not out to scam you.

You can tell me the truth.
Until you tell me how you really found me and what you really
want, I will not respond to you.

Tony

\<rachelp\>	hey mal
\<malFina\>	hey Rachel
\<rachelp\>	what would you do
\<rachelp\>	if a complete stranger wrote you a letter
\<rachelp\>	or called you up
\<rachelp\>	saying that your address or phone # came to them in a dream
\<rachelp\>	and they felt they just HAD to contact you?
\<malFina\>	I guess that would depend on what they wanted from me
\<malFina\>	but I'd automatically think it was somebody I knew
\<malFina\>	or who knew me

\<malFina\>	and was pretending they were somebody else
\<malFina\>	anybody pretending to be somebody else is up to no good
\<rachelp\>	true...
\<malFina\>	why do you ask?
\<malFina\>	did this happen to you?
\<rachelp\>	no, I was just thinking...
\<rachelp\>	unsolicited communication always has an ulterior motive
\<malFina\>	yeah
\<malFina\>	somebody always wants you to buy something
\<malFina\>	or think a certain way
\<malFina\>	to meet their needs
\<rachelp\>	nobody trusts unsolicited contact
\<rachelp\>	except for when it happens face-to-face
\<malFina\>	yeah...
\<rachelp\>	I wonder what makes F2F so different
\<malFina\>	I think it's the eyes
\<malFina\>	people think they can read intention in eyes
\<rachelp\>	yeah. I'm screwed.
\<malFina\>	y?
\<rachelp\>	I'm damned if I do, damned if I don't
\<malFina\>	what do you mean?
\<rachelp\>	he wants only the truth, but the truth is crazy
\<malFina\>	who does? what are you talking about?
\<rachelp\>	I'll tell you in 2 days
\<rachelp\>	by then this thing will be resolved
\<rachelp\>	one way or the other

September 13, 2008

I don't know what I'm going to do.

"Tony" says he's not going to respond to any emails until I tell him the truth about how I found him. Or at least something he'll buy as the truth. I know there's something about him that's important to my brain – enough that his book can calm the humming, and that a number I dreamt about can lead me to his creation.

… Wow. I've been reading that last sentence for the past 5 minutes now, and it's seeming pretty crazy. It makes more sense that I just had a weird dream and generated an obsession over it. Because that's the sort of thing crazy people do.

A random number led me to Moonpulse, and chance and coincidence helped me guess Tony's email address from his book. What could he possibly have for me? He's just some guy! I keep acting like he'll have some important answer for me, but I don't even have any question in mind! Ugh!

Part of me wants to lay it all out for Tony: the exact circumstances that resulted in my first email to him. Now *that* would be a chaos-act if I ever heard of one. How could he not have the same reaction I'm having to this? But why start following Dr. P's advice now?

I'm so screwed. The humming is still there, and I still get a buzz whenever I read Tony's words. Those numbers on my ceiling are still a source of comfort. I can still recite the entire number from memory, and I know every single word of the first 3 chapters of Moonpulse.

To hell with it. Tony gets everything. If I'm gonna be obsessed, I may as well carry it all the way through. I'm such an idiot.

Date: Tues, 14 Sep 2008 14:54:11 -0700
From: rachelP@dystopia.net
To: wolfden@moonlight.net
Sub: The Truth
Parts/Attachments: None

Tony,

You want the truth? Fine. You can have it.
I was led to your book "Moonpulse" – and from there, your
email address – by a number that came to me in a dream. This
number stayed with me every waking hour, gave me comfort
to write out and to say. The first 10 digits are the ISBN of your
book; the rest are a map to the words in your book that make
up your email address. I entered that in a google search, which
led me to the Howler forum.
I don't think I've ever met you or anybody you know, and I'm
beginning to think this has been utter, random chance and
coincidence, the sort of thing that crazy girls like me turn into
the center of the universe and then follow all the way to the
bitter end. While this sort of obsession is new for me, I am no
stranger to mental illness. I know you probably aren't some
incredibly significant figure that will suddenly make me un-
crazy and wash away all the bad genes I've inherited and the
bad choices I've made. You're just the unlucky victim of
chance, and, with this chaos-act, I've managed to tell you both
who you are and who I am.
I'll understand if you don't respond. I'm sorry I wasted your
time. It's a pesky habit of mine – wasting peoples' time with
my crazy shit. I seem to be hooked on it.

My apologies,

Rachel

September 14, 2008

I did it. I wrote 'Tony' and told him the truth. And the dark thoughts are in my bed, on my bathroom mirror, crawling along the floors like thousands of microscopic cockroaches. I can't scrub them all away. It was stupid to think I ever could.

It's so typical of me. A bunch of bad decisions, one after the other, has me in this state of hopelessness, and the beginning of all this was something purely physical, a dream.

Songs of despair and betrayal. Images of falling bodies, splintered bones and blank stares. All because I told the truth to a totally random guy.

Is this the way it's always going to be for me? Am I doomed to keep chasing ghosts of my own invention? Ignoring the good advice of people like Dr. P? Hell, this time I didn't even give Dr. P the opportunity – I knew what she *would* say and chose to ignore that.

Is this the sort of thing that made Mom do what she did?

The humming is gone, and I'm having those ending thoughts again. I know I should talk to Dr. P, tell her everything I've told this journal. But why? What could possibly keep me from relapsing again? This craziness is hard-wired in my brain. The only hope for me is to start over.

But honestly I don't know what would happen if I did it. I'm not afraid of going to hell or anything like that. But what if I got reincarnated as one of those starving kids in the gutters of Tijuana? Or as one of those porno actresses that lets those men defile her in a hundred repulsive ways with a big fucking smile on her face because she honestly sees nothing wrong with it?

It could be worse. I could be a sociopath. In reality, my illness hurts no one but me. Of course, I've worked at that. Grenades don't hurt anybody if there's no one around when they explode.

Sure, it's lonely. But that's the hand I was dealt. The noblest thing to do is to make sure I don't hurt anybody. Who am I to expose people to my craziness when I know the damage it can do? After all, look at what Mom's did to me.

I can't end it. I can't break that promise to Mom. I just have to live with the fact that, every now and again, my brain is going to spout something totally random that I'll either obsess on or get headaches from or what have you, and it will lead me to do something crazy. Hopefully I can recognize it a little quicker than I did this time.

\<malFina\>	so it's been 2 days
\<malFina\>	are you going to tell me now?
\<rachelp\>	tell you what?
\<malFina\>	that stuff about you telling the truth to somebody
\<malFina\>	you said you'd tell me in 2 days
\<rachelp\>	oh that
\<rachelp\>	well
\<rachelp\>	it's a little embarrassing
\<rachelp\>	but I'll tell you anyway
\<malFina\>	I won't tell anybody
\<malFina\>	promise!
\<rachelp\>	ok
\<rachelp\>	there was this guy

\<rachelp\>	and he wanted to know the truth about my history of mental illness
\<rachelp\>	so I told him
\<rachelp\>	even though I knew it would drive him away
\<rachelp\>	it's what my therapist calls a chaos-act
\<rachelp\>	which is an act that just causes needless drama
\<malFina\>	wow...
\<malFina\>	why would he ask about your past like that?
\<rachelp\>	because it was how we met
\<rachelp\>	and it's not just my past, it's my present
\<rachelp\>	and my future

September 15, 2008

There's a snag in my so-called noble plan. And her name is Ynes.

She wanted to do something with me after work today, but I realized that if she and I are friends, I'll just end up hurting her with one of my crazy acts. So I made up some excuse about visiting my father. Yeah, right.

Anyway, I'm stuck: if Ynes and I stay friends, I'm bound to hurt her sooner or later, but if I blow her off, I'll definitely hurt her in a much more direct and pointed way.

Crap. The last thing I want to do is hurt Ynes. She's way too sweet to deserve that. I'd just tell her the truth about how messed up I am, but she'd probably be concerned and want to get me help rather than just see it as an excuse to bail.

I think I might have to move. Not far... Across town, maybe to Peoria or Glendale. Somewhere close enough to still visit Mom on a day off. But I'd tell Ynes that I was moving to

Flagstaff or Vegas or something. To be closer to my father, maybe. Ha.

Moving would be a huge step. But I've got to do the right thing.

I can save enough money to do a move, but I don't think there's any way I could save enough to break my lease. Which means I'm stuck here until December. Maybe Ynes will notice how messed up I am before then and blow me off on her own.

I must be the only girl in the world who hopes her best friend turns on her.

<rachelp>	hi eric
<EIN1104>	Hi Rachel
<EIN1104>	What's on your mind today?
<rachelp>	why do you talk to me?
<EIN1104>	Would you rather I didn't?
<EIN1104>	You can just put me on your ignore list…
<rachelp>	no, I'm glad you do
<rachelp>	I'm just wondering why -
<rachelp>	what do you get out of our little conversations?
<EIN1104>	Well, I've never met you, but in my head you're hot :)
<rachelp>	yeah, right
<rachelp>	seriously, pls
<EIN1104>	OK
<EIN1104>	You have a different way of looking at things.
<EIN1104>	I'm guaranteed to get a new angle on something if I talk to you about it
<EIN1104>	and that's interesting & entertaining
<rachelp>	yeah, a crazy angle
<EIN1104>	heh

\<EIN1104\>	I don't think you're crazy, Rachel.
\<rachelp\>	then it's obvious we've never met
\<EIN1104\>	come now
\<EIN1104\>	You seem pretty sane to me
\<rachelp\>	I'm very good at deceiving people
\<rachelp\>	you're no exception
\<rachelp\>	but back to the point:
\<rachelp\>	so if I were to be boring, you'd stop talking to me, right?
\<EIN1104\>	well, probably
\<EIN1104\>	But you can just put me on ignore if you want me to leave you alone.
\<rachelp\>	no, Eric, that's not what this is about
\<rachelp\>	I'm trying to get this friend of mine to stop liking me
\<rachelp\>	but I don't want to hurt her feelings
\<rachelp\>	so I guess I need to figure out what she likes about being with me
\<rachelp\>	and stop doing those things she likes
\<EIN1104\>	That sounds about right...
\<EIN1104\>	Why do you want her to stop liking you?
\<rachelp\>	it's a long story
\<rachelp\>	but it's for her own good
\<EIN1104\>	Let me guess:
\<EIN1104\>	You're afraid you're getting her hooked on squirrel-watching.
\<EIN1104\>	But I daresay your friend knew what she was getting into when she signed on to that thrill-seeking detail
\<EIN1104\>	She's a big girl, she can make her own decisions.
\<EIN1104\>	hello?
\<EIN1104\>	RAAAAAAAAAACHELLLLLLLLLLLLLLLLL

\<EIN1104\>	I can only entertain myself for so long, you know!
\<EIN1104\>	Ray-Ray-Rachel, Banana-Nana-No-Nachel, Fee-Fie-Fo-Fachel
\<EIN1104\>	Ray-chel
\<rachelp\>	oh god
\<rachelp\>	I just got a really creepy email
\<rachelp\>	I'll talk to you later Eric
\<EIN1104\>	!
\<EIN1104\>	okay – is there anything I can do to help?

Date: Thurs, 16 Sep 2008 09:02:14 -0800
From: wolfden@moonlight.net
To: rachelP@dystopia.net
Sub: re: The Truth
Parts/Attachments: None

God dammit woman, would you get offline already?

Tony

September 16, 2008

Holy shit.

I just got off the phone with Tony. Owner of TEATSFIMB.

Turns out I'm the owner of The *Phone Number* That Sprang From Inside *His* Brain.

He says he had a dream almost a month ago where he was trying to climb down a ladder in the middle of the night but his feet couldn't find the next rung down. He looked at the moon, was hit with a bright flash of light, and then woke up, panting and sweating. And burning a hole in his brain was the number

14802340534

or, MY FREAKING PHONE NUMBER! Those weird hang-ups after one ring were HIM! Apparently he got up the nerve to call a few times, but the strangeness of it all caught up to him as soon as it connected, and he hung up. He thought it was crazy... but ever since I emailed him about how I got his email address, he's been trying to call. But I'm always online, and I turn the ringer off when I sleep during the day, and I don't have an answering machine or voicemail... so he finally emailed me to tell me to get off the internet and free up the line!

We couldn't talk for long – he was using a pay phone, and didn't have much change. He said he'd email me – apparently he's got access to the internet but not to a voice-line. It doesn't make much sense, but he didn't explain. But what difference does it make? This proves I'm not crazy! Or, at least somebody out there shares my shade of insanity!

I'm so happy I can't stop crying! Actually I was crying for most of our conversation. Tony was nice about it, though. He said he knew how I felt: he was pretty sure he was losing it when it felt good to carve my phone number into his skin with his hunting knife. He even got the number tattooed onto his chest - upside down, so he could read it when he looked down. He says that's what finally made the headaches stop.

He said he had to 'take care of something important' but that then he'd email me.

I hope to hell I'm not dreaming!

Date: Thurs, 16 Sep 2008 13:20:49 -0800
From: wolfden@moonlight.net
To: rachelP@dystopia.net
Sub: This past month
Parts/Attachments: None

Rachel,

I can't tell you how relieved I feel after hearing your voice.
This last month I've doubted myself so much that I was
preparing to check into a psychiatric hospital, consequences be
damned. I was sure I'd finally lost it. That 'important thing' I
had to take care of was canceling my ride to the fun house.
But hearing your voice and knowing your story have filled me
with a powerful energy. And that energy has convinced me
that I need to find out how and why our numbers ended up
where they did. We must meet.
I'm willing to go to you – I imagine my lifestyle makes it
easier to suddenly travel across the country than yours does. I
can't go into detail as to why, but it's the same reason I don't
have a phone. Let's just say that I prefer not to give my real
name to anyone for any reason. But I'll tell it to you – we have
enough between us already for me to place some trust in you –
but I'll only do so in person.
I'll leave tomorrow. Please meet me in the Greyhound bus
station in your town. I suspect we'll recognize each other. The
bus will arrive around 3pm your time. Please email me to
confirm this plan. I will not leave until I read your
confirmation email. Please do not include any details of our
meeting in your confirmation.
Something important is happening. I hope you agree, and
agree also that we need to follow through to its end.
Awaiting your response,

Tony

Date: Thurs, 16 Sep 2008 13:42:47 -0700
From: rachelP@dystopia.net
To: wolfden@moonlight.net
Sub: Re: This past month
Parts/Attachments: None

Tony,

I think you're right. Whatever is happening is important. I
think that every now and then the universe talks, and you and I
managed to hear it. We'd be idiots if we didn't meet.
I will be waiting at the place & time you gave me. I will only
wait an hour.
Please email (or call?) if your plans change.

See You Soon,
Rachel

September 17, 2008

I'm nervous. Gee, I wonder why - I'm only about to go to a bus
station to pick up a guy I've never met, have spoken to only
once, and who claims my phone number came to him in a
dream, which has been driving him crazy for the past month.

It seems insane on its face, but it *feels* right. The humming
sound is gone. It's now a buzz that has my limbs glowing with
warmth and my eyes full of lightning swirls. Apparently I was
singing as I did the floors at work today. Ynes said something
about how pretty my voice was. I don't remember singing,
but it wouldn't surprise me if I was. I was flying.

But...

My feelings have betrayed me before. I remember this sort of mania with Derek, with Randy, and especially with Dr. McCarty. And all of those guys were complete disasters. I don't think 'Tony' is like any of them... but I still feel like trusting him is the most natural thing to do.

I'm going with it. I have to. I can't fight how right this feels. I'm off to the Mesa Greyhound station. With any luck 'Tony' won't kidnap & torture me for a week before leaving me to die in the desert somewhere. Heh.

September 18, 2008

His name is actually Curtis Benzel. And he's HERE. Dyeing his hair in my kitchen sink as I type.

He was easy to pick out at the bus station. He was the guy in the denim jacket looking around him like he was expecting a dozen cops to descend on him from the rafters.

Before I could say anything to him, he rattled off my phone number. I replied with my 34-digit monstrosity. It was the first time I'd ever said it out loud to anyone (on purpose). I felt an odd sort of relief when I said it, like I was confessing.

We went straight to my car, and Curtis's dark eyes darted around the entire time. He explained that he hadn't been in Arizona for 7 years, and so he had no idea how 'safe' he was here. Whatever that meant.

He finally relaxed when we got to my place and I showed him the numbers on my bedroom ceiling. That's when he showed me his tattoo. It felt like comparing scars. Only we really weren't proud of them.

We talked for a long time. Unfortunately we have a lot in common when it comes to mental illness. Things went south for him later than for me, apparently, but we've both had multiple stays in psychiatric hospitals. And St. Luke's – the one with the church steeple in Tucson that had supposedly inspired him – well, it inspired him because he was a resident there. It's really called Santa Lucia... and I know I did some time there. It's the only real link we could find between us, and an unpleasant one at that. It's obvious that something happened to Curtis there – his eyes tear up and he bites his lip just at the mention of the name.

As for me, I don't want to remember. Those memories are sealed away with a bunch of dark thoughts, and it's taken me a long time to get away from them. I don't want to let them out of their cage.

We both hated the idea of going back to Santa Lucia. And so we agreed that was precisely what we had to do. Curtis closed his eyes for a long time, then said he'd only go if he dyed his hair.

I can feel tension between and around us, like we're both in the same powder keg. But we're both certain that whatever brought us together is now pointing us to Tucson, to Santa Lucia.

Why? Who knows? Maybe aliens will land there once we step on the grounds. Maybe there's a safe with a 45-digit combination that nobody's been able to crack. I don't know.

But I know I have to go. I just hope I can do this without unlocking any of those bad memories.

We leave after I get back from work tomorrow. Curtis is staying here, on my couch. He hasn't tried to touch me, or turn our meeting into any 'written in the stars' romantic BS. I really appreciate that.

Besides, imagine our kids. They'd wear little Napoleon hats in the womb.

\<rachelp\>	hey mal
\<malFina\>	hey rachel
\<malFina\>	how are ya
\<rachelp\>	good
\<rachelp\>	listen
\<rachelp\>	I'm sorry I've been so shady lately
\<malFina\>	don't worry about it
\<malFina\>	are you okay?
\<rachelp\>	I don't really know...
\<rachelp\>	I'm going to go back to the scene of some really bad stuff
\<malFina\>	why?
\<malFina\>	that's bound to be painful
\<rachelp\>	I know... but I have to
\<rachelp\>	I met this guy, and he's got his own bad shit associated with this place
\<rachelp\>	and we both know that we've got to go back
\<malFina\>	I thought you didn't trust men
\<malFina\>	you told me you had irrefutable evidence that they were all liars
\<rachelp\>	this one's probably a liar too
\<rachelp\>	but I know he's not lying about this
\<malFina\>	so what are you going to do when you get to this historic place?
\<malFina\>	burn it down?
\<rachelp\>	dunno
\<rachelp\>	haven't got that far yet

<malFina>   well, you'd better think of something
<malFina>   or else your festering history will boil over
                    inside you once you reach your ground zero

---

September 19, 2008

As soon as Curtis wakes up, we go back to Santa Lucia. And I'm a nervous wreck.

My voice was shaking when I told Ynes that I had to leave town for a few days. When she asked why, I explained that there was something in my past that I had to attend to. She said she could see in my face that I was going to slay some demons. She said she admired me for it, and that she'd make sure my shift was covered. She's amazing.

She started to give me a hug, but I darted away like a mouse. She said she'd give it to me when I came back.

I don't want to go. I don't see what good could come from opening that cage of memories. They're too strong. They'll just overwhelm me. And Curtis, too.

But everything inside me tells me to go. Why else did Curtis come here? Why did my phone number appear in his head? Why did I go through the ordeal with his book?

I'm so scared. It's one thing to lose your sanity; it's another to see the plunge off the deep end coming. And to take steps toward it.

Curtis probably feels the same way. Maybe he's just waiting for me to give him a reason to bail out.

God, I hope so.

Date: Sun, 19 Sep 2008 17:04:51 -0700
From: guestuser12@acacia.lib.tuc.gov
To: rachelP@dystopia.net
Sub: dark thoughts
Parts/Attachments: None

I don't know what the hell Curtis is thinking.
He talked me into driving to Tucson with a lot of "we can get through this together" bullshit. I gnawed on my finger the whole trip down. It's a bloody mess.
But Santa Lucia isn't there anymore. There's a fucking mini-mall in its place. Curtis had to make sure, though. He went inside and asked the owner of the dry cleaners. Said Santa Lucia was torn down in '02. But Curtis didn't want to go home. He says we were at the right place, just not at the right time.
So now we're at the library. Curtis is looking at microfiche of old newspapers. I don't know what the fuck he's expecting to find. But he says he's good with libraries. Says he spends a lot of time in them because it's the only way he gets on the internet.
I want to go home. I can't take this feeling, this pressure coming from everywhere around me. It's like I have both of my hands pressing down on the lid of a barrel full of roaches. It takes all of my energy to keep it shut, and even then I see roaches scuttling along the floors out of the corner of my eye. But every time I look, they're gone. Like in the old times.
I can't keep this up. I'm going to explode. But no, Curtis is fucking determined. He has this grim look in his eye, like he's marching off to war or something.
He's calling me…

Tucson Reporter, August 20, 2001

INVESTIGATORS CALL SANTA LUCIA INCIDENT
'SUICIDE BY COP'
by Martha Mulrooney

TUCSON -- Initial findings indicate that the victim of
Thursday night's police shooting at the Santa Lucia
Psychiatric Hospital wanted to be shot, a spokesman for
the Tucson Police Department said today.

Lieutenant Jason Peterson said that the victim, Manuel
Boroquez, advanced on police with a syringe full of
glass-cleaner even after repeated hits with pepper-spray.

"The victim shouted the word 'máteme', which is
Spanish for 'kill me.' He said it over and over again,"
Peterson said.

"He left our officers with no choice but to defend
themselves with deadly force."

When asked why, if he wanted to die, Boroquez didn't
just inject himself, Peterson said that Boroquez couldn't
be sure that the cleaner would do the trick.

"He knew that gunshots would end his life. He couldn't
be too sure about the contents of the syringe," Peterson
said.

Santa Lucia is a treatment center specifically aimed at
teenagers with severe emotional or psychological
problems. Boroquez's file was not made public, but

Peterson said the 19-year-old had a history of self-destructive behavior.

The investigation should be complete by the end of the week, Peterson said.

The funeral for Boroquez will be held at Citizen's Cemetery on Sunday.

September 21, 2008

I opened the cage. And I'm still alive.

It was quite a scene at that library in Tucson. Curtis broke down, sobbing onto my shoulder. Apparently he'd blacked out in Santa Lucia one night, then found himself in an alley a few blocks away, covered in blood. There were police and ambulances everywhere, and he'd had problems with violent behavior before, so he was convinced he'd done something awful. He started running, and never really stopped.

He'd actually been attempting an escape independent of Manuel Boroquez's hostage/suicide-by-cop plan. But Curtis had convinced himself that he'd hurt someone while blacked out – he couldn't be sure whose blood was on his hands. He says he remembered that he just scraped his hands on the ladder when he heard the gunshots. But that memory was covered up, buried deep inside him until he read the newspaper report detailing the events of that night. All that werewolf fascination makes a lot of sense now.

So Curtis was feeling absolved, but I was still a shivering wreck from trying to keep those dark thoughts in their cage. But Curtis told me that had to be the reason we had the dreams – to get us to remember that specific night and deal with whatever really happened. I begged, I pleaded with him just to take me home, that I felt like tearing my eyes out and carving holes in my feminine organs, and that it was up to him if I lived or died.

Curtis got us out of there before my blubbering brought the cops. I thought we were going back to the highway, back to Mesa, away from that terrible place.

But he drove me to a cemetery. To Citizen's Cemetery.

I kinda shut down then, just sorta stared into space as the cockroaches crawled up and down my legs, in and out of my belly button. Curtis dragged me out of the car and physically carried me to Manuel Boroquez's grave.

And when I saw his name on the headstone, I remembered.

I remembered what that orderly was doing to me in the hallway that night. I remembered the roach crawling along the edge of the dirty tile floor. I remembered the paperback that had fallen to the floor, how the words were just barely out of focus, and thinking that if I could just get a little closer I could read the words on the page and that would distract me from the orderly, from his sticky hands, his awful, sweaty stench. But I couldn't read it. All I had to look at was that dirty floor and that cockroach crawling along it.

Then, the gunshots.

I remembered it all, and I sobbed onto Manuel's grave. Curtis kept his hand on my shoulder, gentle, like he was saying "I'm here, but this is something you need to do on your own."

Eventually I look up for a breath, and there's two other girls there, both crying on Manuel's grave. They were too overcome to speak, but one of them choked out "Dream… number… Santa Lucia."

Then I recognized them: they were both in the girls' wing at Santa Lucia with me back in '01: Rosie and Farrah.

They both had dreams about a month ago. Rosie dreamt about a shower and woke up with Farrah's house number, apartment number & Illinois zip code stuck in her head. Farrah dreamt about a darkened cafeteria and woke up with Rosie's Texas driver's license ID number in her head. And there they were. It'd taken them about a month to convince themselves they weren't crazy, contact the other, and make their way back to Tucson.

The four of us talked all night, in the dark, on Manuel Boroquez's grave. We dug up our demons and had them dance for our new friends.

Santa Lucia was a horrible place with horrible people running it. But it took what Manuel did to draw attention to the evils inside. Rosie told me that half the '01 staff was in jail six months after Manuel was shot. All four of us were long gone by then. We were already damaged when we went in there, and by the time we got out we were all broken.

Curtis was a paranoid nomad, Rosie was a junkie some of the time and co-dependent all of the time, and Farrah was obsessed with some of the sickest sexual stuff I've ever heard of – punishment was a big theme for her. And then there was me, the isolationist who couldn't clean enough floors. We were all fucked up.

And then we all had a dream that took place in Santa Lucia, on the day when Manuel begged a cop to shoot him. And we all somehow had numbers stuck in our heads that connected us to somebody else that was in the building that night. Turns out it was seven years to the day between the dream and the event we dreamt about.

We're all certain that Manuel did it again, somehow, from beyond the grave. It's funny, I don't even remember his face, but I feel like he's given me a huge gift.

The four of us had lives to get back to – well, except Curtis – so we exchanged information and promised to stay in touch. And promised to visit Manuel together every seven years. I might do it more often. I think I'll look up his family and pay them a visit too. I hope they speak English.

Anyway, I gave Rosie and Farrah big hugs, and my skin didn't crawl. It glowed.

The next morning Curtis turned himself into the police. He doesn't know how long he'll have to serve for escaping a court-ordered psychiatric stay, but he said it didn't matter. It will be worth it to be able to live honestly again, and some state mental-health treatment probably wouldn't hurt. I gave him a big hug too, and told him to call me when his release day was up. He shouldn't have any problem remembering my number.

I go back to work tomorrow feeling like a new person. I called Dr. P and told her to reserve two hours for me this week. I've got a lot to talk about.

By no means am I cured. I still have my problems. But without that sealed cage of dark thoughts to worry about, it feels like an underlying cancer is gone. I just have to rebuild my immune system now. And I've got three friends around the country who know exactly what I'm going through.

September 22, 2008

Ynes gave me that hug today, and I gave it back. It was wonderful.

Tomorrow morning after work I'm going to tell her all about my last month, and I'm not afraid of how she'll react. I know it will be positive, because she's my friend, and she loves me.

Maybe she'll come with me to translate when I find Manuel's family. Maybe she'll tell me what happened to Lencia.

I'm going to call Rosie, make sure she made it home all right. She said she wasn't great at the computer, but she could handle a cell phone with the best of them.

I bet I can hang with her.

<rachelp>	hey eric
<EIN1104>	yo
<rachelp>	I just wanted to say
<rachelp>	thanks for being there for me
<EIN1104>	being where? Sacramento?
<rachelp>	no… I mean for listening to me
<rachelp>	I know I can be difficult to put up with
<EIN1104>	pleasure's all mine, rache
<EIN1104>	you're not planning anything drastic, are you?
<rachelp>	no!
<rachelp>	*NO!*
<rachelp>	far from it!
<rachelp>	I'm just feeling grateful for a lot of things lately
<rachelp>	today it's you
<EIN1104>	gosh, rache…

<EIN1104>   you've got me blushing somethin' fierce
<rachelp>   good :)
<EIN1104>   you sure you're ok?
<rachelp>   yes
<rachelp>   I can honestly say that I've never been surer.

An Act of Mercy

"JUST A COUPLE MORE TURNS, SOLI."

She groaned, so I flipped on the dome-light and stole a look at the backseat. Soli lay on her side with her face pressed into the vinyl of the seat-back. Her legs were curled up, and I could see the dark patch on the small of her back where the windbreaker bunched up. The bloodstain looked about the same as it had twenty minutes ago. Maybe the bleeding had finally stopped.

Thick stands of pine flanked Route 77 behind low banks of day-old snow. I don't know what I would've done if the road hadn't been recently plowed; there was no way my old Skylark was ever going to climb any snowy mountain switchback. The curves all looked the same at night, but I had a landmark to watch out for: a lightning-split gray oak in the crook of a hairpin turn. The bare branches finally appeared, so I pulled onto the next dirt road, plowing through four inches of untouched accumulation.

I bounced along in second gear for a half-mile or so until a cabin appeared on the left. It was an unlit shack with no power line running to it, just a blotch in the darkness of the forest.

"We're here."

62

Soli didn't say anything. Her body was perfectly still.

I touched her leg: it was hard and cold, like a refrigerated egg. "Soli?"

She groaned again and turned onto her back. Her chocolate-brown eyes squinted against the dome-light.

"All right Soli, I'm gonna carry you. It's gonna hurt, but we have to get you inside."

She swallowed thickly, nodded, and closed her eyes.

I opened the door, and the cold quickly penetrated my thin denim jacket. We needed a fire right away.

Soli was lying on a fleece blanket, which I wrapped it around her as I prepared to pick her up. I expected her to cry out as I lifted, but she didn't make a sound. Nor did I hear the slightest peep as I carried her through the snow. I could feel her shallow breaths through my chest.

The interior of the tiny cabin was just as cold as the night outside. The single bed was covered with dust, but I laid her on it anyway. That fire had to come soon.

"It hurts."

"I gotta start a fire, Soli. Hang in there."

I switched on the battery-lantern hanging by the door. Newspaper and kindling were stacked neatly beside a wood-burning stove, and in a few seconds I had a decent fire going. I tossed in a couple of logs from a pile in the corner and closed the cover.

"Nicky…" She said my name softly, like she was talking in her sleep.

"Okay, Soli. Let me take a look at your side."

I held the windbreaker open and gently pulled up her sticky white blouse. The bandage was black with dried blood, but there was no fresh crimson seeping down her back. That was a good sign. I carefully peeled back the surgical tape and lifted the gauze.

There was nothing there, just Soli's olive skin. The gash that had run from her hip to her ribcage was just gone.

I ran a fingertip over the downy hairs where the wound should've been. Not a good sign.

Soli groaned again. "Nicky, it hurts." Her dark eyebrows slowly knotted together, like she when smelled sour milk. "It hurts so bad."

"Yeah, it's a pretty good cut." I knew perfectly well what was hurting her, but maybe she didn't. "How 'bout some morphine for the pain?"

She nodded. "Yes, yes, please."

I had three loaded syringes in my jacket pocket. I flicked the air bubbles out of one as she snaked her arm out of the windbreaker.

Her body relaxed as I pressed the plunger. When I removed the needle she rolled over onto her back. She looked right at me with wide, clear eyes.

"It's happening, isn't it." She could've been reciting a pizzeria phone number.

I shook my head. "You're gonna be fine. You just need some rest."

"Please don't lie to me, Nick."

I set my jaw. "You're not gone yet. Get some sleep. I'm gonna make some calls, find out what the hell happened back there."

She stared at me for a couple of heartbeats, and then closed her eyes. In a few minutes she was asleep.

I took a deep breath. The adrenalin from the drive was wearing off, and energy was melting out of my arms and legs. The knot between my shoulders began to ache again, and my hands were sore from gripping the steering wheel. I sat on the floor in front of the stove and warmed my stinging fingers.

That gash in Soli's side should've needed a dozen staples to close. I hadn't imagined it - the bloodstain was proof enough of that. Had she bled too much? Was the change happening?

Soli sighed and turned over. I pulled my cell phone out of my pocket. I had to take advantage of her morphine-rest while I could.

THE NIGHT ALL THIS STARTED I DECLARED I WAS GOING to drink until I forgot about Tracy, the latest girl to leave me.

Specifically, I needed to forget her kiss-off speech, and how similar it was to the ones given by Emily, Jessica, and by a half-dozen women before that. I apparently didn't "have any goals," I wasn't "going anywhere," and was "wasting my potential." It was like women all read from the same script. I wondered if they practiced their lines together in clandestine weekly meetings.

I don't remember much of it, but apparently I put on quite a show at my buddy Buzz's place. I think Buzz liked having me at his parties just for my post-break-up raves. I usually subjected anyone near me to a fun combination of confessional, poetry and sermon.

This killer redhead played along with me, fed me lines, hung all over me. She looked like something out of a beer commercial, all legs, cleavage and smile. Eventually she drew me out of Buzz's front door while the festivities were still in full swing. She wanted to know where my car was.

"Lady, I couldn't drive anywhere to save my life."

She smiled, and the orange streetlights sparkled in her blue eyes. "I don't want to go anywhere. I just want some privacy."

I grinned and led her around the back of Buzz's house to the dirt alley where I was parked. But then I remembered that Buzz had my keys. He'd known about my plans to get profoundly hammered and confiscated them from me when I arrived.

I relayed this fact to the redhead – I couldn't remember her name – with my apologies. She took a long look around the alley and smiled.

"That's okay, Nick. This will do just fine."

She grabbed me by my shirt and tossed me against the alley's brick wall. Before I could catch my breath, she kissed me, long and slow. She inhaled deeply, as though she was trying to taste the air in my lungs. I don't really like the crack-the-whip type, but her hair smelled like oranges and I was eager to be distracted from Tracy's clichés.

But then the redhead bit my lip, hard enough to break through my drunken haze.

I pulled away and put my hand to my mouth. Warm blood dripped down my chin. "Jesus, lady! What the hell?"

Then I saw that her eyes weren't blue anymore. Two tiny scarlet orbs glowed beneath her arched brows, like the taillights of a late-model Impala.

She smiled, which revealed her fangs. They were long and curved, like a rattlesnake's.

"Are you scared yet, Nick?" The words slithered from her mouth in a hiss. "I like it so much better when you're scared."

My entire body jolted, like when you suddenly wake from a nightmare. But she was still there, running her purple tongue up and down her glistening fangs.

She lunged at me, and I managed to raise my arm; so instead of my neck, she sank her teeth into my wrist. The pain was incredible, but my lungs wouldn't empty when I tried to cry out.

She pulled my arm aside and effortlessly pushed my chest to the wall. My limbs weren't responding to my brain's urgent pleas. I couldn't even close my eyes to avoid witnessing my own violent demise.

She winked at me, and then opened her mouth to finish the job.

But before her fangs reached my carotid artery, something crashed into her side and she tumbled to the dirt.

The something was actually a squat Hispanic man with a goatee. He and the vampire rolled around in a patch of street-light, grappling over what looked like a two-foot-long piece of PVC pipe.

"Run!" the man yelled.

I took his advice. But I tripped on a rock as I staggered into the darkness. I waved my arm to brace myself, but the pain from the bite locked my elbow in place. My head thumped against something hard, and everything went black.

I FLOATED THROUGH OUTER SPACE, WEIGHTLESS, SILENT. Pinprick stars drifted by, and I tried to wave hello to them but my arms wouldn't move.

One star was winking at me. I drew closer, and the brilliance filled my vision, flashing on and off. I was certain it was communicating to me in Morse code: "T-h-e-r-e i-s l-i-f-e..."

And then the light was gone, and blackness surrounded me again.

"Can you hear me, Nick?"

The light returned, but it wasn't a star – just a penlight shining into my eyes. A hand drew it back, and I saw a blurry form: dark hair, eyeglasses.

"Mngh," I answered.

"You're in a safe place." It was a man's voice. "Do you remember what happened?"

The left side of my head throbbed, a tire-iron pounding my skull in time with my heartbeat. "I don't know why Jansen hit me so hard," I mumbled. "I didn't even have the puck."

"Come again?"

"I was trying to get from second to third, but I'd already handed the ball off to the tailback. That's gotta be a flag. Fifteen yards, automatic first down!"

"I can see you're still a little confused. I want you to rest here, but don't fall asleep, okay?"

I nodded. "Whatever you say, coach."

"Your lip looks fine, but I need to check this puncture wound on your arm. Does it hurt when I-"

"Ow!"

"Right. Believe it or not, that's good news. Take these pills, they'll help with the headache."

He put a pair of tiny pink pills in my hand along with a paper cup full of water. After I swallowed, I could see him a little better: he wore a black dress-shirt with the sleeves rolled up. I wondered where his white coat or scrubs were.

"What was your name, doc?"

He scribbled some notes onto a clipboard. "Phygrxla."

"Huh?"

"Castrlyunh."

I blinked. He smiled. "How 'bout I tell you an hour from now, when you've recovered some of your senses?"

"Deal."

"I have to check on another patient, Nick. I'll be back in ten minutes. Those pills ought to keep you awake, but even so, do not fall asleep. You got that? Just rest here."

"Right. No sleeping for Nicky, as per the orders of Doctor Whosifudge."

He grinned, shook his head and left the room.

The pillow was soft and cool on my cheek, and I had to bite my injured lip to stay awake. I was still wearing my familiar jeans and t-shirt, but my sandals were missing, which made the bed even more comfortable. The room was narrow and windowless, but bright with fluorescence. I wondered why I had my own room. And for that matter, where I was.

As the pounding in my skull began to ease, I remembered being at a party with Buzz. But everything was a blur after the fourth shot of Jagermeister. I figured I got super-bombed and smacked my head on something, and somebody had been nice enough to call an ambulance. Maybe I'd ended up in a rich-people hospital in Scottsdale where even drunken head injuries get their own room. That would explain the comfy bed.

There was no way I could pay for all this. I made a mental note to give Dr. No a phony address when asked.

Then I felt a severe pressure in the area of my bladder, and it occurred to me that if I did not find a toilet soon I would make this comfortable bed a nasty-smelling place. And there was no toilet in this room.

I swung my bare feet to the tile floor and slowly stood up. My knees buckled; they seemed to think I was spinning on a merry-go-round. I took tiny steps and leaned against the bed, and managed to make it to the door without falling.

The dim hallway was lined with thick, midnight-blue carpeting, which felt nice on my toes but seemed odd even for a Scottsdale hospital. I also couldn't find any of those lit signs along the walls or ceilings that normally direct drunks like me to the X-ray lab or the gift shop. Or more importantly, to the restroom.

On the bright side, slouching along the narrow hall cleared away most of the dizziness. My room was at the end of a hallway with no windows, so I was fairly confident I could find my way back again. It was okay that the rooms weren't numbered. I probably couldn't remember numbers anyway.

I stumbled along the wall, pleased with myself for creatively applying the doctor's orders to stay awake. When I reached an intersection I heard some commotion from down the adjoining hall.

Suddenly a young woman turned the corner, checking behind her shoulder before running straight at me in a blur of olive skin and blue jeans. I guessed she was probably in her early twenties, but I've always been terrible at that kind of thing. She didn't even look at me as she darted down the hallway I'd come from.

"No pisser that way," I slurred at her back. "Just a dead end."

Then two more people turned the corner in her wake: Dr. Whatshisface and a pale woman with orange-lens glasses. They were running toward me just as the girl returned from the dead end.

They all converged on me and stopped, panting. The olive-skinned girl was holding a knife. Seeing no escape, she held the blade to her throat.

"C'mon now," Dr. Pribibbila said. "Let's not do anything rash."

The girl shook her head. Her black hair swayed about her shoulders like a gentle breeze pushing heavy sable drapes. "There's no point," she said brokenly. "How can I live, knowing what I am?"

"Listen to us," said orange-specs. "There are lots of us living fulfilling lives with this condition. Nothing has ended. Yes, your life is going to be different, but - "

"But you're still alive," I finished. "And where there is life, there is hope."

Everyone looked at me as though noticing me for the first time. Dr. Tibbyslipslip waved at me to get away, but then the olive-skinned girl dropped the knife. She fell to her knees and covered her hands with her face. Orange-specs crouched and put her arm around the distraught girl's shoulders.

The sobbing made me sad so I turned away, just in time to see a squat Hispanic guy with a goatee. He was leaving a room from which I could hear that wonderful, unmistakable gurgle of a toilet finishing its flush.

"Thank Christ!"

I shouldered my way past the familiar-looking man and into the bathroom. Dr. Molybdenum called my name as I closed the door, so I promised him that I wouldn't fall asleep while I peed. He banged on the door, yelled something about not leaving my room. I told him to hold his water, that I'd just be a minute.

I washed up and opened the door. The doc looked at me like I was a misbehaving puppy, just barely too cute to drop-kick. I grinned at him.

"Hello, Nick," he said tiredly. "I'm glad to see you're feeling well enough to move around. Do you remember anything more about last night?"

I nodded. "Yeah, I was at Buzz's party, and I got destroyed. I think Mr. Jagermeister had a lot to do with it. Oh yeah, and I met this hot redhead."

I noticed the bandage around my wrist for the first time. And then I remembered how I got the wound.

"Why don't we go back to your room and talk," Dr. Carmelcorn said.

I swallowed hard. "Yeah, why don't we."

AFTER I WARMED UP A LITTLE, I PULLED A DUSTY PONCHO out from underneath the bed and draped it over my shoulders. Soli murmured in uneasy sleep.

"Back before you know it," I whispered.

I ventured back into the night, retrieving a pair of old work gloves and a flashlight from the trunk of my car. Then I crunched up the side of the mountain.

I knew there was a line-of-sight cell phone tower on top of a nearby hill; it was just a matter of getting high enough so my signal could escape the trees around me. The forest wasn't thick, and I made sure I didn't lose sight of the lantern glowing softly through the tiny back window of the cabin.

My shoes and socks quickly became soaked with snow. There was still no wind, but my ears stung and my nose was running. It was hard to believe that Phoenix's heat and sprawl were just a few hours' drive away.

When I finally got some signal bars, I pulled my glove off and dialed.

"All-Nite Cleaning Crews answering service, this is Stephanie, how can I help you?"

"Hey Steph, it's Nick. Can you talk?"

"One moment, sir." I heard a click, and then Steph's voice lost its neutral professionalism. "Nick, thank God! Are you all right? Where are you?"

"I'm okay. I'm on the Fort Apache Rez near Show Low, in a safe place. Soli's with me, but she's hurt pretty bad. I gotta talk to Dr. Prybyszewski. Has he checked in with you?"

"Yes, he wasn't at the Orphanage, thank God! He and some others are heading north somewhere to regroup. Prescott, I think."

"I really need to talk to him. I'm afraid Soli doesn't have much time left."

"Hang on, let me get you his cell number."

I shivered in the dark, bouncing my legs to keep the blood flowing. I had to get back to that fire soon. "Steph?"

"Yeah?"

"What the hell happened at the Orphanage? Who were those guys?"

She sighed. "Well, we don't know much. All the reports I've received say the intruders were all human. No uniforms, no official vehicles, but their grenades were military issue, and they sure knew where they were going. I've got fourteen confirmed lost." Her voice quieted to a hush. "They got Luis, Tamara, Calvin, Necole... God, they killed Jessie! She was just fifteen! What the hell did she do to deserve this?"

Of course I had no answer, so I didn't say anything. I just watched my breath steam from my mouth.

"Jesus, Nick! It - It's all over, isn't it?"

"I don't know, Steph." I thought about all those people, friends of mine, comrades in the fight against their awful condition. They were just gone. I felt tears forming in my cold eyes, but I bit my lip to fight them back. I had Soli to worry about. "Do you have that number yet?"

She sniffled. "Yes." She gave me Dr. P's digits.

"Thanks, Steph. You should probably leave the valley, you know."

"No way. I have to keep the lines of communication open. And even if anybody did come after me, my cover's fine."

"All right. But you be careful."

"You too."

I ended the call and jogged through the hardpack to the cabin. I needed the fire, and I couldn't let Soli wake up alone.

BACK IN THE EXAM ROOM, THE DOC LAID IT OUT FOR ME. Yes, that thing that bit my wrist was a vampire. They'd been in Phoenix since the population explosion began in the 1960's. No, this wasn't a hospital; it was the 'Orphanage,' a safe house for people who may have been infected by the vampires. If one of them injects its venom into you without killing you, then you've got ten days of humanity left before sunlight turns you into a pile of dust bunnies.

No, I wasn't infected. Yes, the olive-skinned girl with the knife was.

But the people at the Orphanage offered hope for the freshly infected. If they found you within that ten-day window, they could stall the vamping. He didn't tell me exactly how that was done, but the victim ends up sort of in-between. 'Orphans' still have their human soul, but their bodies crave blood, dissolve in the sun, are burned by crucifixes and so on. Just not as badly as a full-blown vamp.

"So that girl in the hallway..."

The doc folded his arms. "Her name's Soledad."

"She'd just found out she was infected."

He nodded.

"What's gonna happen to her?"

"There's no cure," he said flatly. "But we can neutralize the progression. There are dozens of us living semi-normal lives with the infection. It takes a lot of discipline, but you can survive for years without going over the edge."

I blinked. "Us? You mean you're - "

"Going on four years now." He ran a hand through his black hair, and I noticed the dark lines beneath his eyes. Like someone who didn't get much sleep. "The craving is always there, but as long as we avoid temptation, we keep right on living. The real danger is accidents. The closer the body gets to death, the harder it is to resist going full-blown vampire. It's like some kind of defense mechanism."

I didn't say anything. Not only did I suddenly live in a world where vampires existed, but I'd damn near become one of them. It was quite a load for my hung-over brain to absorb.

I nodded stupidly as Dr. P told me I was out of the woods for my head injury and that he thought I was healthy enough to go. They'd call me a cab, and would I be good enough to keep their existence a secret?

"Nobody would believe me anyway," I mumbled. I remembered the pain in Soledad's eyes. She had an awful secret now, one she'd have to keep for the rest of her life. That easily could've been me. Her tortured voice echoed in my mind: *How can I live, knowing what I am?*

Dr. P walked me downstairs, through a narrow foyer to the front door. Between the knock on my head and the lack of windows, I was surprised to find a typical sunny desert day taking place outside.

A brilliant grassy lawn ran up to 20-foot privacy hedges that bordered each edge of the property. I took a quick look around and found North Mountain looming to the west. It all told me I was in one of the older neighborhoods in North Phoenix, where the houses were built far before the days of gravel landscaping and miniscule side-lawns. This wasn't a safe house. It was a safe mansion.

I shook my head. "Doc, I owe you big, but I barely got two nickels to scrape together."

He smiled. "We don't do this for money, Nick. Forgive me if I don't walk you to your cab."

I nodded and shook his hand, but didn't walk outside. I just stared at the wheels of the taxi idling on the driveway. The back passenger tire sagged, seeming to melt where it touched the concrete. That was about how I felt: underinflated.

"Come on, Nick," Dr. P said as he turned away. "Surely you've got people worried about you, wondering where you've been all day."

I shrugged. "Not really. But I won't take up any more of your time. Thanks again."

I stepped into the sun. The warmth was pleasant; I imagined the sun dissolving a film from away from my skin. It occurred to me that none of the occupants of the house could feel this warmth. They probably never would.

"Hey Nick."

I turned back. Dr. P was cleaning his glasses with his shirttail. "If you have some time, we could use your help."

HE SENT ME TO COSTCO.

I took a nine-passenger van and filled it with refried beans, flour, soda, dishwashing detergent, bug spray and a bunch of other household items, all in bulk sizes. I was nervous at the checkout, but the clerk didn't even blink when I gave him Dr. P's credit card.

Dr. P was waiting for me in the garage with his sleeves still rolled up, along with a tall dude with shoulder-length brown hair named Ronnie. We unloaded and stowed the Costco stuff in the kitchen. Just as we finished, Dr. P begged off, saying he had some patients to see upstairs. Before he left he gave me a lanyard with a laminated card that read "NORM" in big red letters.

"My name's not Norm. It's Nick."

"It's not your name, it's what you are. Wearing this lets everybody know you're fully human. That way we don't think you're trying to off yourself when you step into the sunlight."

"Right."

He shook my hand. "Thanks for helping us out, Nick. You're welcome here at any time. Ronnie will call you a cab when you're ready to go."

He took off, and I looked at Ronnie. He had that same sleepless look about his brown eyes: the pinkish whites, the purplish lines above his cheekbones.

"So," I said. "Are you, uh..."

He raised one of his dark eyebrows. "Fighting the impulse to rip your throat out and use your trachea like a straw to suck up all that delicious blood swirling inside you?"

"Actually I was about to say 'going to watch the game,' but if you have anything you need to tell me, please go right ahead."

He blinked. "Oh, you mean Cards-Cowboys? Hell yes!"

"Is that to the game, or the trachea-straw?"

He grinned and showed me into the den. It was a small room with cheap wood paneling, a modest television and a couple of old but comfortable couches.

Already lounging on one of the sofas was a short, stocky guy wearing a red baseball cap. His eyes carried that sleepless look, but with an extra glaze of drunkenness.

"Jake, Nick," Ronnie said. "Nick, Jake. Nick's a new Norm, and he's gonna watch the game with us."

Jake nodded. "'Cards or 'pokes?"

"Cards."

"Damn right," Jake said. He raised his Coors in a toast. "The perpetual underdogs. Just like us Orphans!"

So we watched the game, occasionally yelling at the Cardinals' terrible run defense and their inability to catch a pass. During commercials Ronnie explained that the two of them worked nights cleaning offices in the hi-rises downtown. It was hard work, but it was a living.

They both hoped to advance up to 'agent', the Orphans that patrolled the streets at night, looking for vampires. Like Luis, the guy who saved me from being that hot redhead's dinner.

At halftime I asked where I could find Soledad, and Ronnie told me that all the recently-orphaned stay on the second floor for a month while they adjust to the infection. "But you should probably leave her alone," he said. "She's been a little... What's the word I'm lookin' for?"

"Bitchy?" Jake suggested.

"Upset," Ronnie said. He shrugged. "Can't say I wasn't pissed when I first got infected. Forced to spend a month quarantined here, cut off from whatever life you had, knowing that life was over now. It sucked. You should probably give her a few days to calm down."

"That sounds like a good idea," I said, standing up. "But why start following good advice now?"

I found her room upstairs at the end of another of the narrow hallways with the thick blue carpet. I softly knocked on the door, which opened at my touch.

Soledad sat at a tiny table shoved against a wall, staring intently at a blank piece of paper. A pen rested in one hand and the other gripped her forehead. She didn't look at me.

"Um, hi, I - "

"I have to call my parents," she said quietly. "I need to feed them a story so they don't file a missing persons report. Tamara said I should write out what I'm going to say so they don't catch me in a lie." She twirled the pen along her thin fingers. "So did I just meet some boy that swept me off my feet, carrying me away from everything I've worked so hard to earn at the university? Or do I now have a drug problem? I wonder if I'm whoring myself out for cash yet." She covered her eyes with her hand.

"Wow, that's hard," I said lamely.

She moved her hand but still didn't turn to look at me. "You know I've never lied to my mother once. Not even about boys."

I didn't say anything. I just watched her spin her straight black hair around her finger in furious knots.

"Listen," I finally said, "I'm really sorry about earlier. I didn't mean to be crude at a sensitive time for you. I was, y'know, recovering from a head wound. Didn't really know what I was saying."

Soledad nodded, but kept staring at the blank page. "Do you feel better?" she asked.

"Yeah, the doc gave me some pills."

She shook her head. "No, I mean now that you've apologized to me. Did this make you feel better?"

I blinked. A tear slid down her cheek, and it may as well have been a drop of napalm burning a hole through my stomach. "No," I answered. "Not really."

She sniffled. "Me neither."

"I'll quit bothering you."

I closed the door, pressed my back to it and let out a deep sigh. "I should probably give you a few days," I murmured. "To calm down."

TURNS OUT THERE'S NO QUIET WAY TO STAMP YOUR FEET, but I tried to do it anyway that night in the cabin as I warmed up in front of the fire. Soli stirred and rolled over. Her breath was quick and shallow.

Her arm was cold to the touch, so I lay beside her to share some of my body warmth. It was like hugging an ice sculpture.

"Come on, Soli," I whispered into her hair. "We're not licked yet. We can beat this."

She wheezed. "You've got to... do it, Nicky."

I bit my lip and drew her cold flesh closer. "No."

"I can't survive... a cleansing," she gasped. "You've got to... end it."

I blinked the tears away and pulled the second morphine syringe from my jacket.

"Just relax, Soli. You'll feel better. I promise."

I HUNG AROUND THE ORPHANAGE A LOT OVER THE NEXT few weeks. I did anything they wanted: trips to the bank, to the MVD, even helping out in the yard, trimming those huge privacy hedges. Everybody seemed really grateful that I did these ordinary things, which made them even easier to do. In the mornings I played video games and shot the shit with Ronnie and Jake; eventually I switched my shift at Safeway to nights, so I could hang out with the Orphans more. I didn't really miss my prior hazy evenings with Buzz and the crew at the Block and Tackle. After a while I stopped going out altogether.

Soledad was still at the Orphanage, generally in her room, sometimes in the kitchen. I made a point of being nice to her. It felt like the right thing to do, like maybe if I showed her enough kindness my chest would stop aching whenever I thought about her.

But she wanted nothing to do with me. One day she physically threw me out of her room, and I splashed the vegetable soup I'd brought all over the hallway carpet. As I scrubbed the blue shag with stain remover I heard a voice:

"She doesn't want your pity, Nick."

I looked up. It was the lady with the orange-lens glasses, Tamara. She'd helped run the Orphanage for almost fifteen years, but her smooth face and thin frame belonged to a woman of twenty-one. Unnatural youthfulness was apparently one of the less unpleasant side effects of the infection.

I shrugged. "I just feel so bad whenever I'm around her. It could've been me in her spot real easy."

She nodded, tucking a lock of black hair behind her ear. "That's survivor guilt talking, Nick. I've seen it in a dozen Norms before you. We appreciate all your time, but you aren't responsible for what happened to Soledad. You don't owe her anything."

"I know. I just wish I could so something to help her."

Tamara put her hand on my shoulder. Her fingers were ice cubes through my shirt. "Try treating her like a person," she said, "and not like a victim. That's all any of us want."

I stopped my scrubbing and stared at Soledad's door. I didn't have any trouble treating Ronnie and Jake like 'people,' but Soledad was obviously different. And maybe that wasn't fair to her.

Tamara excused herself, and soon all of the second floor residents quietly filed out into the hallway and padded down the stairs. Even Soledad came out, passing me with a roll of her eyes.

Curious, I followed them downstairs. Everyone was congergating in the great room, but when I tried to follow through the double doors, Dr. P stopped me.

"Sorry, Nick. Cleansing, Orphans only. Be a dear and answer the phone if we get any calls? And fill up the mop-bucket. Just in case."

"Oh. Sure, sure."

I didn't have any idea what he was talking about, so I pretended to search for the mop in the kitchen while keeping one eye on the hallway leading to the great room. As soon as those double doors closed, I crept up to them and listened.

I heard Tamara's muffled voice, then Dr. P's, but I couldn't make out what they said. Then I heard a bunch of voices chanting in unison:

"We beseech you, oh Zera: cleanse the craving from our tainted blood."

Then silence.

Then a collective gasp, like everyone in the room had been kicked in the shins.

Moans. Sobbing. Cries of torment. An audible wave of anguish, steadily growing louder. Was this supposed to be happening? Did they need help?

The sound kept coming, kept crashing into my ears. Two dozen shrieks blended together, and I thought for certain that I was hearing the howling winds of Hell itself. What possible help could I be against that?

I just stood there for a minute or so, listening to all that pain, and that hole in my stomach flared up again.

Finally the wave of sound crested, and the cries faded to quiet sniffles. The doors burst open, and who runs into me but Soledad, her hands clutching her stomach, her face gray and drawn. I tried to stumble to one side, but we ended up bumping chests.

She then threw up on my shoes.

When she finished spitting she glared up at me. "Always in the way," she gasped.

I started to yell an apology as she hurried away, but I caught a sour whiff of her vomit. I had to close my mouth to keep my lunch from joining Soledad's on my shoes.

Dr. P clasped my shoulders. "Got that bucket, Nick?"

**

79

I WRAPPED THE PONCHO AROUND SOLI'S SHOULDERS AND rubbed her back. "Thank you, Nicky," she murmured.

Her kiss was cold on my cheek, like a pair of frozen green beans had replaced her lips. "You're welcome," I said. "So you're warming up some?"

Her eyes rolled under half-closed lids. "No, silly. I'm thanking you for my lovely present."

I squinted. The fire crackled as a log shifted to the back of the stove. "What present is that?"

She twirled a finger in the air. "This present. This *now*. You bought this for me with all your hard work. I just want you to know that I appreciate it. To spend a few last moments with you, here, in safety, rather than..."

"No, Soli." I threw the blanket aside and climbed out of the bed. "I haven't given up on you yet. We can still find a way out of this."

She pulled at her black hair, and her eyebrows scrunched together. "No, Nicky... I'm too scared. I'll miss my heart, or not get the stake through my ribs, and that will spark the change, and I - "

"I'm not killing you, Soli!"

I bit my lip at my outburst. I squeezed my hands into fists, and then grabbed the cell phone off the tiny wooden table. "I'm gonna call Dr. P. He'll know what to do. I'll be right back."

She pitched forward, gripping the poncho in her hands. "Nicky, please don't leave, I'm scared - "

"I'll just be five minutes. You can hold on for five minutes, right?"

She held my gaze as a tear slowly ran down her cheek. The burning pit in my stomach erupted. But she nodded.

"Good. I'll be right back."

As soon as I opened the door I remembered that the poncho was still in Soli's hands. But I plunged into the cold anyway. I could take five minutes of shivering.

I reached the call-spot again and dialed the number Steph gave me.

"Yeah?"

"Dr. P, thank Christ! It's Nick."

"Nick? Jesus, where are you?"

"I'm in the cabin on the Fort Apache Rez. The one you had me stock up last month. Soli's with me, and she's really hurt."

"Oh yeah?" I heard the *click-clock* of a turn signal in the background and figured he was in a car. I wondered how long our connection would last. "How hurt?"

I described her cold body, how the wound in her side had vanished, and how she was afraid that a cleansing would kill her.

He sighed. "Nick..."

"I'm not going to stake her, doc. Give me another option."

"Well, she's right. At this point the shock of a solo-cleansing would kill her. But that'd probably be doing her a favor."

A gentle breeze whistled through the trees, but there was nothing gentle about the Ginsu-grade blades of ice running across my nipples. "Doc!"

"Yeah, I know, not gonna kill her. Well, we've been experimenting with a Norm-sharing method with a little success. I suppose it's worth a shot."

I staggered a crazy jig to keep my extremities from going numb. "Any p-port in a storm, doc. What do I do?"

"Just hold her hands during the chanting. She knows the words, but the morphine makes them hard to remember, so you'll have to wait until the drug starts to wear off. You'll share the intensity of the cleansing. It's gonna hurt like a sonofabitch. But Nick, you have to promise me something."

I wiped my mouth; trails of snot had frozen to my upper lip. "What's that," I said.

"If this doesn't work, you have to end her suffering. We can't have another vampire running around. And just imagine how scared she is that she'll turn into a monster."

"D-Don't worry, d-doc. I'll make it work."

"Nick! Promise me you'll kill her!"

"Gotta go, doc. My nuts are freezing off."

"God damn it, Nick! If she kills anybody after she turns those lives are on your - "

I ended the call and sprinted back to the cabin. Of course it would work. I could take any pain compared to the thought of killing Soli.

"SON OF A - !"

Grease from the frying bacon popped and spat onto Soledad's fingers and forearms. I was stocking the cabinet below the sink with dishwashing detergent and sponges, so I could see her bite her upper lip in frustration.

"God motherfucking – ah!"

I snickered. She glared at me. She bent her short body to turn the knob on the range without getting burned again.

I smacked my lips. "Mmmm, fried Soli fingers. Them's good eatin'. You put some barbecue sauce on there, n' you'll be - "

"Shut up!" she yelled, and punched me in the arm.

But she was smiling. And man, was it ever a smile! Bright teeth behind full lips; round cheeks pinching to an adorable pair of dimples; flashing chocolate eyes despite the dark patches beneath them. It was the first time I had seen Soledad smile, and I felt something cool and fizzy where that burning hole in my stomach used to live.

"Hey Soledad," I said. "Go out to dinner with me."

"Yeah, right," she smirked. She flipped a piece of bacon. "It's hard enough to not make *you* be my dinner."

She licked her canine teeth at me, but I shrugged it off. I was used to the Orphans' black humor. Ronnie and Jake occasionally referred to me as 'Delicious Nick.'

"No, really," I said. "Dr. P said you can go outside now, right? It'll be fun. And you might run into somebody who knows you. It'd be good for the cover story."

She frowned and wiped her hands on a washcloth. "I guess. But why go with you?"

"Because I'm the one asking you."

She rolled her eyes. "And why should I say yes to you?"

"Because I'm not asking you as Nicky the Norm." I gave her my cheesiest grin. "I'm asking you as Nick Perkins, the great guy who just got blown away by your fabulous smile!"

She shook her head, but she was smirking. "No way, Nick. Never in a thousand years."

We went out that very night. I can be pretty persistent when it comes to women.

HER DARK EYES DARTED BACK AND FORTH, AS THOUGH Soledad expected the restaurant to burst into flames at any moment. Her fingers tore at the bread crusts on her plate, and her jaw was clenched as she ground her teeth.

"Are you all right?" I asked. My cell phone rested on the table next to my wine glass. I had the Orphanage on auto-dial in case Soledad freaked out, and I was checking in with Tamara every half-hour. I also had some loaded morphine syringes in my jacket pocket. It was the only way Tamara would let us go out without an Orphan chaperon.

"I'm okay, it's just..." Soledad's eyes darted back and forth, then she leaned in close: "I can smell everyone in this room."

"Oh yeah? Are they good smells?"

She nodded. "Tempting smells. Craving smells. It's very distracting."

I wiggled my eyebrows suggestively. "What about me? Do I smell tempting? Eh?"

"No, you smell like cheap cologne."

I grinned. "I might just survive the night!"

She rolled her eyes, but couldn't hide her smile. She recrossed her legs and glanced at the oil paintings of cowboys, horses and lassos along the walls. "I've never been to a Carver's before. Are you sure you can afford this?"

I nodded. "The Orphans have been feeding me every day for the last few weeks, and I've been so tired from my night job at Safeway and hanging with Ronnie and Jake that I haven't been going out much at all. I'm pretty stacked right now. For me, anyway."

"Wow, you mean you actually have a bill in your wallet that has double digits?"

"Yeah, you think they take pesos here?"

We laughed.

Her filet mignon arrived – cooked rare, of course – and she attacked her meat with decidedly unfeminine enthusiasm. I thought it was cute, and said as much. She rolled her eyes again and asked if I'd rather she went after my neck.

With Soledad relaxed, I kept up the goofy charm while I gave her the Cliffs Notes version of my life story. Grew up in North Phoenix, always had lots of friends, especially after my Mom died when I was 12. Did okay in school, went to Glendale Community College for a while, but they didn't offer any classes in carousing, so that didn't last long. Almost got engaged once, but the girl turned out to be a psycho.

I didn't mention the kiss-off speeches. I also avoided talking about the Orphanage or anyone there.

As she chewed, Soledad told me about growing up in Mesa. Her parents owned a couple of Mexican restaurants, and she hated working in them. But now she was going to ASU to get a business degree so she could help her parents with their money. She loved her family and wanted to help, just as long as she didn't have to be around shredded beef or margaritas.

Her eyes clouded over as she reminisced. "You know, every Cinco de Mayo all the Montoyas picnic in this little park in our neighborhood. The kids play soccer, and my little niece Clara always wants me to push her on the swing. I guess that's all over now."

"Not all of it," I said. I did my best to ignore the burning in my stomach; I knew the pain had nothing to do with the ribeye I'd just finished. "You don't have to disappear from your family entirely, right? You can still be part of Clara's life. You can still be that cool aunt who really knows what's up, you just have to do it over the phone. You can even see her in person, as long as the sun's down. Right?"

"I guess." She stared at the filmy streaks of congealed blood on her plate. "The nights are all I have left." She sighed.

"Nights aren't so bad." I gazed intently at her shiny eyes. "Ever been to Turret Peak at night?"

She shook her head. I turned on the cell phone. "There's something there that you should see."

**

WE HIT THE HIGHWAY AS SOON AS WE LEFT THE RES-
taurant. I drove her north up Interstate 17, past Anthem, New
River, and Black Canyon City. Soledad stared at the road and
didn't say much. I kept yapping, just trying to stall until the right
exit appeared.

Eventually she said, "If you're heading for a make-out place,
you've got the wrong idea. It's not happening."

"That's fine with me. After that redhead bit me I'm a little
leery of liplock. I just want to show you some of the great things
that the night is capable of."

She shook her head. "You know, I'm getting a little sick of
your cheery attitude, Nick."

"Too bad. I got no other way to be."

My exit finally came, and I turned off the highway onto a
Forest Service road. But Soledad wasn't done: "Must be easy for
you to be so damn optimistic when you're surrounded by cursed
people all day."

I shrugged. "I do have a new appreciation of how lucky I am.
But I appreciated life long before I met any of you Orphans." I
downshifted as the dirt road sloped uphill and pine branches
scraped along the sides of the Skylark. "My mother died in an
auto accident. Really sudden. Nothing I could do about it. It
showed me that life can be taken away in a heartbeat, so we've
got to live while we're still alive. You're still breathing, right?"

She rolled her eyes. "There are worse things than death, you
know."

"But you're breathing."

She sighed. "Yes Nick, I'm breathing."

"Then you're still alive. If you're still breathing, you're still
living. And where there is life..."

Soledad's head jerked up. The dashboard lights twinkled in
her dark eyes. "...there is hope," she finished. "Where have I
heard that?"

I swallowed my smile and stopped the car. "Dunno. But
we're here."

'Here' appeared to be halfway up a mountain along a Forest Service road in the middle of nowhere. Pine trees blocked out most of the night sky, so I left the headlights on when we exited the car. I retrieved a flashlight from the trunk, as well as my old Cactus High windbreaker, which I tossed to Soledad. She stared at the tires while she absently pulled the jacket over her shoulders.

"That was you," she said softly. "'Where there is life, there is hope.' You said that, at the Orphanage, when I was about to – you know."

"Yeah, I guess I did say that. This way."

I followed a narrow hiker's path into the dark of the forest. Soledad hurried to catch up. "So are we in search of some buried treasure of yours, Nick? Please tell me you don't have a dead body out here. That's the wrong kind of gesture for someone with a blood craving. The idea is to fight my urges, not give in to..."

She trailed off because we'd reached a clearing on the crest of a hill. The land dropped off steeply a few feet in front of us, revealing the desert vista on full, panoramic display.

The moon was new, and the mountains shielded us from the Phoenix light pollution; all we saw were stars. Hundreds of thousands of stars spelled out constellations familiar and foreign in the dry desert sky like countless tiny snowflakes frozen in midfall. Directly above our heads a Milky Way stripe ran across the horizon like a white, cosmic tire-track.

I pointed the flashlight upward. "Not buried treasure," I said. "More like the opposite."

Soledad crouched in the deergrass and swiveled her neck to take it all in. "Wow."

I sat beside her and clicked the flashlight off. The wind was still, and Soledad's sniffles were all I could hear.

"Wow," she said again.

I nodded in the darkness. "My mom used to take me here when I was a kid. I remember getting so bored that I'd just throw rocks off the cliff as I waited for her to finish staring at the sky. When I would ask her what she was looking at, she'd always say

'I'm watching the night.' I didn't get what she meant till years later. But by then she was gone."

I heard Soledad breathe deeply, and then her hand found mine. She was cold, but I didn't let go. "See?" I said. "Nights aren't so bad."

She swallowed. "Not so bad."

She gripped my hand tightly, and we just sat there, watching the stars move across the sky.

"Nick?"

"Yeah?"

"You can call me Soli. That's how my family knows me."

"Okay, Soli."

"Where did you get that life and hope phrase?"

"I'm not sure. I think it was a Star Trek episode."

She lay back into the grass. "I think I liked you better when you had a head injury."

"That's what Dr. P said."

IMAGINE A RUSTY THUMBTACK WEDGED INSIDE YOUR wrist. Imagine it scraping along the inner wall of a vein as your blood pushes it up your arm to your shoulder, into your heart, through your belly and then down each leg. Imagine the jagged path that tack would tear through your body.

Now imagine a hundred thumbtacks shredding your insides as they slash through every vein and artery.

That's the sort of pain I shared with Soli as I held her hands in the cabin. Piercing agony everywhere. In my fingernails, my eyebrows, my testicles, the soles of my heels. Everywhere.

Like a sonofabitch.

And then the pain vanished, as though a flood of ice water had quenched all the fires inside me. I opened my eyes: I was still cross-legged on the bed with my hands outstretched. But Soli was in a quivering ball on the floor, her fingers clutching her sides. Her lips squirmed as she gasped again and again.

I dropped to the floor, and from my knees I could see her half-opened eyes. Tiny lines of blood danced across the whites like red bolts of lightning across a milky sky – but the bolts remained, layering atop each other as they made their way toward the iris. The gasps became a low, steady moan, and she bared her teeth. The canines were longer, and I thought I could see them growing.

I quickly pulled out the final syringe and flicked away the bubbles. I watched her eyes as I injected her arm. The blood slowly retreated from her irises, but remained swirling around the perimeter. The moans stopped and she looked at me.

"Couldn't take the pain," she gasped. "It felt like my heart... Exploding."

"That's okay," I said softly. Her hair was sticky with sweat, but I stroked it anyway. "I know you tried your best."

Her cold hand wrapped around mine. "Do it now, Nicky. This is the last chance."

Cold tears filled my eyes. "No," I said. "There's got to be something else we can do. I'll call Dr. P again."

She rolled over and weakly punched my leg. "No. It's over. You have to."

I shook my head. "I can't lose you, Soli. Not if something can be done. Especially if I have to be the one to kill you."

"This isn't about you!" she cried. She opened her mouth to say more, but coughs erupted instead. "I don't want to become a monster, Nicky," she said, blood trickling out of the corners of her mouth. "Please don't do this to me!"

I climbed to my feet, but I didn't turn to face her. "You're going to be fine, Soli. I'll be right back."

"No! Nicky!"

She clawed at my jeans, but I shook her off.

"Please! You've got to kill me now!"

I grabbed the cell phone and dashed out into the icy night. If I really was going to shove a wooden stake through the heart of a woman whose smile could make me climb mountains, I was going to be damn certain that there was nothing else I could have done. She wasn't gone, not yet. As long as she kept breathing, we still had a chance to get out of this mess.

As I slogged through the snow to the call-spot, I could hear her plaintive cries, just above the wind: "Nicky..."

I didn't look back.

WE HIT EVERY GREEN LIGHT ON THE WAY HOME FROM Turret Peak. Soledad - Soli - chatted animatedly about her nieces and nephews. She wanted them to know enough of the truth about vampires so they would never end up dead or Orphaned.

I pretty much let her talk. I liked the sound of her excited voice.

We neared the Orphanage, and Soli asked me to drive in the back way, down the paved alley that the garbage trucks used.

"So you're ashamed to be seen with me?"

"You're not as dumb as you look." She grinned and stuck her tongue out at me. "Actually, I just know that Tamara is going to give me the third degree as soon as I get in. But I'd like to get some sleep before I give her my report on being an Orphan amongst humans again. If we go in the back I might be able to slip into my room before she sees me."

"You're the boss."

I turned the car into the alley and killed the lights, then made a joke about how the only vehicle less stealthy than a Skylark had to be a Winnebago. We stopped at the back wall of the house next door; I was going to leave the car there as we hopped the neighbor's chain-link fence and sneaked through the privacy-hedge to the back door.

I wonder where I'd be now if I didn't go with her.

We got out of the car and quietly closed the doors. Soli looked at me over the roof: half of her smiling face glowed orange in the streetlight. The other half was lost in the darkness.

"Thank you for a wonderful evening, Nick the Great Guy," she whispered.

"You're welcome," I whispered back. "Did this make you feel better?"

She cocked her head. I didn't realize until later that I had repeated her scathing question from our first conversation. But she just gazed at the hood, a tiny smile playing at the corners of her mouth. "I think... I think I'm gonna be okay."

We were three furtive steps past the privacy-hedge when the garage exploded.

The blast emptied my lungs as it threw me back into the hedge. I blinked through the falling grit; the ringing in my ears obliterated all sounds except my breathing. What just happened?

From the light of the burning garage I could see dark figures advancing from the driveway and from the back gate. White lights blinked before them as they moved.

As my hearing slowly returned I heard the gunfire, and realized that the lights were muzzle flashes. The Orphanage was being raided. And the attackers weren't taking prisoners.

"Soli!"

I found her sprawled under the hedge in a puddle of bloody grass. Her teeth were clenched, and her hands gripped a dark stain on her side. I didn't see any of the muzzle flashes advancing in our direction, but I figured it was just a matter of time before they saw us.

I made my decision.

"YEAH?"

"Dr. P? It's Nick again."

"Nick? Hang on a second." I rubbed my tingling forearms and ran in place; I never took my eyes from the cabin. "How'd the shared cleansing go? Hurt like a sonofabitch, right?"

"It sure did," I said. "But Soli couldn't handle it. Said her heart was exploding."

"Oh." His tone became somber. "Then I trust you did the right thing. Well Nick, I know everybody here admires you for trying as hard as you did, but it just wasn't meant to - "

"I didn't stake her, doc. I gave her my last morphine shot."

"What? She's still alive?"

"There has to be something else I can do."

"Damn it, Nick, the only thing you can do is put her out of her misery! Maybe if she were here, where she could share the cleansing with the twenty of us that remain, then you could do something. But you're way out in the middle of - "

"Nowhere, right. But you had me set this place up for a reason. Isn't there something here that could help her?"

He snorted. "Yes, the pile of kindling. You can make a pretty good stake out of..." He trailed off.

"Doc? You still there?"

"Say, Nick. Did you stock the cabin with any alcohol?"

"Yeah, I brought a bottle of tequila, but this is hardly the time to drown my sorrows."

"No, listen to me! You have to get Soli to drink the tequila until she passes out. If you're going to save her, then you have to get her to us; if she's going to survive the trip here, she's got to be in a coma of some kind, and alcohol will have to do. If you have anything sweet to cut the flavor, mix it in – we can't have her throwing any of it up."

He took a deep breath; so did I, filling the air before me with my steam. I knew there was a way!

"Now, given the night's events," the doc continued, "we have to assume that the valley is unsafe, even to drive through. So you'll have to head north to I-40, through Winslow. That's going to be a long trip through the mountains, probably six or seven hours, so make sure you tie Soli up in the trunk before you go. And don't tell her where we are! If, God forbid, she escapes from you, I don't want her knowing where we're hiding."

"Okay, but I don't know where you are. Steph said Prescott, but she wasn't sure. Is that right? If so, where in Prescott?"

No response.

"Doc?"

The phone's display read "CALL DROPPED." I quickly pushed the redial button.

I crashed to the ground before I could hit send.

Something was on top of me, spreading my arms apart and pressing my elbows into the snow. Strands of soft, damp hair raked across my eyes and poked into my mouth. I felt hot breath on my neck, and then a wet kiss.

And then screaming pain, a cold, filmy liquid entering me while my warm blood drained away.

I tried to struggle, but Soli was now much stronger than I was.

SOMETHING COLD AND WET TOUCHED MY FINGERS, AND my eyes shot open. I was lying in the snow, and as I bolted upright, something heavy and itchy slid off of my face. After a couple of blinks, I saw a startled coyote retreating into the forest. The old poncho rested in a pile on my lap; it had been covering my face.

The sun was halfway to noon, glittering brightly off of the sheet of snow covering the ground. I was lying in a shadow of an oak tree; the cabin was just down the hill. I hadn't moved far from the call-spot, where Soli...

I put my hand on my neck. It was stiff and tender, but I wasn't bleeding, and I apparently hadn't frozen to death. I fingered the itchy poncho. So she'd spared me?

I shook my head. This was better than I deserved. I'd let her become a monster, a fiend, because I was too weak to do what had to be done. But she'd shown mercy to me. I didn't think those things were capable of mercy.

I started to stand up, but my fingers suddenly stung, like I'd pressed them to a hot stove burner. I fell back to the snow. What the hell?

Then I put it together. My fingers had left the shadow of the oak when I tried to stand. They'd been burned by the sunlight.

I swallowed hard, and my bowels suddenly felt cold and sticky. I couldn't see the car, and my cell phone was apparently gone as well. And I had ten days to somehow find the Orphans - who may or may not have been hiding out in Prescott - to keep myself from ending up like Soli. Prescott was halfway across the state, and I was sitting on top of a mountain in the middle of nowhere without communication or transportation.

And then there was Soli. I had no idea where she was. I wondered if she was standing in another shadow, watching me rub my wounded neck and bury my burning fingers in the snow.

Either way, I knew she wasn't happy with me.

I carefully climbed to my feet and steeled myself for the sprint through the sunlight to the cabin. I needed that tequila real bad. I hoped Soli had left it for me. Now that would have been an act of mercy.

Hope & Dez

"TO HELL WITH HOPE!"

Chris had no destination in mind. Dark highways, dim streets, bright parking lots. His muscles drove the car while he ruminated.

Why did she always leave when he needed her the most? Five days ago he visited his father in the hospital, and when he returned to his apartment Hope was gone. So were her rings, her perfume, her shampoo, everything. Like she'd never been there.

This wasn't the first time Hope had vanished on him. She was never gone for long, and Chris couldn't remember her reasons for leaving. But tonight he was sick of waiting for her to come back. He had to do something, go somewhere.

The car stopped on an unlit residential street. The shapes in the darkness were familiar, like furniture in a darkened bedroom.

Pear Street. Of course, Chris thought. Lights never worked for long around Dez.

Chris wondered if he really wanted to be there. Hope always came back, but if she found out he'd been with Dez...

But now he was at Dez's door. His finger found the doorbell in the darkness. Well, he conceded, Dez was always happy to see him.

The door opened.

Dez looked better than he remembered. A smooth black dress hung from her shoulders, hugging her thin waist like a socialite cradling a champagne glass. The garment matched Dez's hair perfectly: Chris couldn't tell where one black ended and the other began. Her pale skin glowed faint orange from her tinted lampshade, her dark eyes were steady.

"Christopher. I'm glad you're here." Her thin lips barely moved.

"I'm sorry, were you going somewhere? I can come back."

"I am always here for you, Christopher." She closed her eyes halfway and bowed her head. It was the closest Dez came to smiling. "Come in."

Chris stepped across the threshold into a mist of jasmine, sandalwood and apple. Dez guided him to the couch, a leather beast that swallowed him into someplace cold. He held his hands to the fireplace, but the lazy flames did not warm his fingers. The fog of incense and Dez's unexpected beauty were both distracting. Why was he here?

"Hope's gone," he said.

"I know." Dez sat across from him and poured a couple of white Russians into tumblers on the lacquered coffee table.

A couple of sips chased the fragrances and dizziness from Chris's head. The sofa warmed: the beast had turned its belly to the sun.

"Her absence is the reason you are here, yes?"

He nodded. "And I really need her right now. My job's become dead-end, a childhood friend just moved out of town, and my father..."

Chris recalled the hospital bed, the sour-smelling food, the attractive nurse whose beauty somehow made everything worse. And his father's eyes, filled with pain and fear.

"And where the hell is Hope?" he said. He held his hand out like he was testing for rain.

Dez swallowed. "She has left you before."

Chris nodded. "But she was always back in a day or so. Sometimes less."

"How long has it been?"

His glass was empty. "Five days."

"Five days," Dez whispered. She leaned closer, and her dark eyes pulled at him like undertow. "You don't deserve to be abandoned like this."

Chris was no fool. He knew Dez carried a dim torch for him, a spot of darkness held aloft in a sun-bleached, shadowless desert. But Chris had wanted Hope for as long as he could remember. He loved Hope's smile, her laughter, her bright, happy eyes. She got along so well with his friends, her body moved so easily when they danced. He and Hope made a great pair, but she kept vanishing at the worst times.

Dez, however, would always be there.

Somehow his glass went from empty to half-empty, and his chest warmed. "You'd never leave me, would you Dez?"

Somehow she was beside him, her pale arm encircling his shoulders. "Of course not."

Sure, his friends hated her, but Chris could rely on Dez. She would always be there when he needed her, always listen, always hold him like this.

He wrapped his arm around her bony side. That arm went numb, and Chris felt a similar blankness grow in his mind. The little things weren't little. The bricks he felt on his shoulders weren't bricks. They were his bone and flesh stacked upon him, bending him earthward. He had no doubt that Dez would be there to catch him when he crumpled.

Chris wondered why he had no doubt.

Black eels swam in his eyes, blotting out Dez's dim living room.

His throat felt like it was lined with velvet. "What do you want, Dez?"

Her breath was cool on his warm neck. "I thought that was obvious, Christopher. I want you. All to myself."

Chris had never gone all the way with Dez, and an important part of him wondered what it would be like. He was certain, however, that Hope would know he'd done it. And then he would never see her again.

He clenched his right hand, the one he could still feel, into a fist. Something cold touched his fingers, and he turned his palm to look.

The ring. A thin silver band with a polished sapphire. It'd been on his hand so long that he didn't feel it any more.

It was a gift from Hope.

He remembered the day she gave it to him. She sent it to his office on a Tuesday, five months away from his birthday. She called him to make sure he received it.

"I put myself into that ring, you know," she'd said. "So every time you look at it, you're really looking at me."

How had he responded? "Yes, I can see you in it now. You're sticking your tongue out at me."

"I'm doing what?"

He blinked. Dez was looking at him with her head cocked. Orange specks of reflected fire danced in her pupils.

Her fingers paused in their exploration of his ribs. The eels in his vision hesitated.

Chris grasped Dez's cold wrist. "I'm sorry, Dez. I don't think I'm ready to give up on her."

Dez nodded. The eels evaporated and his arm returned to him. "Very well," she said, as though placing a drink order.

"I should go."

Standing made Chris's head swim, and the mist of jasmine, sandalwood and apple made him cough. He felt his way around the couch.

"I will always be here, Christopher," Dez said.

Chris smiled. "I don't think you'll be lonely without me, Dez."

He made it to her door, which stuck on the first pull. Chris looked back before crossing the threshold, and Dez was still sitting on that leather couch, orange, dark, sympathetic, consuming.

"*Au revoir*, Christopher," she called. "See you next time."

Chris thought of Hope's smile and how much he missed it. He wanted to fire back with "No, this is our last good-bye," but the words wouldn't come. So instead he smiled, shrugged, and turned away.

Pear Street was colder than he remembered.

An Easy Target

"I DON'T THINK YOU UNDERSTAND," THE COUNSELOR
said. "I'm saying that you can't go back home. Ever."

I shrugged. "Fine by me."

**

8/4 20:00

Patient 561 presents with sweats,
vomiting, inattention and confusion. Pulse
122, BP 83/60. No obvious wounds or open
sores. Preliminary evaluation indicates
classic syndrome response. Order 50 more
ccs Phenergan and fluids.

Patient is adolescent male, anglo, brown
hair brown eyes. Arrived with no
identification or personal items.

```
Patient not combative, has not asked for
family or friend.

                                    -T. Pearsall
```

**

"MY NAME IS LUIS," THE THICK-CHESTED MAN SAID. "I'M A counselor and I'm here to help you. I don't know how much you remember, but you've been through a traumatic experience and my job is to help you cope with what's happened."

I didn't say anything. I was surprised to see that he didn't have a notepad or a tape recorder. The office was small; I sat in an almost-comfortable plastic chair. My IV stand stood beside me like a street light on wheels.

"What's your name?"

"Devin," I told him.

"How much do you remember, Devin?"

"All I remember is puking over and over again. For like six hours."

"Okay," Luis said. He had a dark goatee, and the right side of his lower lip flinched for a second, touching the hairs above his upper lip. "How are you feeling now?"

I shrugged.

"I see." His lip twitched again. "Well, would you like to know where you are?"

I shrugged again. "Doesn't really matter."

"That's actually a response I hear a lot from people in your situation." Here came the notepad, out from under his chair. But he handed it to me. "If you feel like writing anything down, you can use this. Sometimes the anti-nausea drugs can mess with your head, and this way you can write your thoughts down before they fade away."

"Why would I want to do that?"

"Because the more you remember, and the more we understand what happened to you, the easier it will be for you to heal."

"What if I don't want to heal?"

He smiled. "We'll see about that."

**

Entry 1

Finally stopped yakking, which is nice.

This room is small but it's got a TV and a crapper, and I'm by myself, also nice.

Note to whoever is reading this while I sleep: I'm ready to go home now.

**

"SO I'D LIKE TO GO HOME," I SAID. I GESTURED TO THE IV stand. "Could you get someone to pry these tubes out of my arm?"

Luis frowned. "You're not ready to go home yet, Devin. You haven't been cleared medically. And we haven't even started on dealing with the trauma yet."

"I can take care of myself."

"Don't you want to know what happened?"

"I'll figure it out. And if I don't, so what? I just want to go home."

"Did you know that you were covered in blood when you were admitted here? And you don't have any injuries, so the blood wasn't yours."

I blinked. Blood? All I remembered was puking. "Did I hurt someone?"

He nodded.

"Bad?"

He nodded again.

I tried to think, but the time just before the puking was like a huge gray cloud in my mind. Concentrating on it did nothing to clear it up. "Am I in trouble?"

"You could be," Luis said. "We're not sure what the authorities know at this point."

"What did you tell them?"

"We haven't told them anything yet."

Yet. The word echoed in the room as it bounced around my mind. So that was the deal. If I don't play along, they go to the cops and tell them I did something terrible. "What do you think happened?"

He shrugged. "We have our guesses."

I raised my eyebrows. "And?"

"We don't want to pollute your memories with suggestions. What I've said about being covered in someone else's blood we witnessed for ourselves, but that's about it. The rest we want you to remember on your own."

"Uh-huh." Crap. Did I need to come up with a story? I didn't know what they knew.

"We don't have it in for you, Devin," Luis said. "We just want to help you deal with what's happened to you."

I stared at the pale blue carpet. "I really don't remember anything besides puking."

"I'll help you with that. We'll start slow, and gradually detail will come back to you. We'll use kid gloves."

"Can we start tomorrow?"

"No problem."

**

Entry 2

Boned.

It's apparently Friday morning, and the last thing I remember is going to the store on Tuesday. And now I'm in a hospital after apparently hurting someone really bad. I don't have any bruises or cuts or anything, but there was blood all over me when I got here. Or so they say.

And they may or may not go to the cops with all this. If they haven't already.

Truth is, I do want to know just what the hell happened, why I'm sick, why can't I remember 72 hours or so. But I don't want to be manipulated.

Luis seems all right, but I don't know his intentions.

So yeah, I'm boned. But that doesn't mean I'm not going to be careful.

**

"Let's start with the basics. Do you remember how old you are?"

"I turned eighteen three months ago."

"Did you attend high school?"

"North Valley. I graduated last month."

"Oh, congrats."

I shrugged.

"Do you remember where you live?"

"Sunset Vista development on the north side."

"Who do you live with?"

"My mother."

"Do you remember her name?"

"Yes."

"If you don't want to tell me, that's fine. I just want to know that you know."

I nodded. He didn't ask for my address. I liked that.

"Do you have a job?"

"I work part-time at the library. Data entry, shelving books."

"Do you like it?"

I nodded. It was true. "I like things to be organized."

He nodded. No notepad. His dark eyes were focused on me, but not with any creepy intensity. "You mentioned that you live with your mother. What about your father?"

"Never knew him. He apparently died when I was nine, but he wasn't real involved."

"Okay. What are your future plans? College?"

I bit my lip. "I don't really know. I was just trying to get through high school."

"Okay." He scratched his chin. "When I was your age I just wanted to go wherever my friends were going. What do your friends have planned?"

My back suddenly itched and I had to bend my body awkwardly to scratch it with my thumbnail. "My friends aren't really in the same situation."

"How so?"

"They're not in high school, so..."

Luis raised his eyebrows. "How old are your friends?"

I shrugged. "Some are older, some younger."

"I see." He crossed his legs. "It must have been hard going through high school without any friends."

My face got hot and I clenched my fists. "I didn't say I don't have any friends."

"And I didn't say you didn't. But none of these friends went to high school with you."

I stared at the carpet. Who has carpet in a hospital?

"Am I right?"

I sighed. "My best friend Marcus moved away just before high school started. And, I don't know, it just sort of never happened. Getting by actually wasn't that hard. I got real good at being invisible. If you don't give anyone any reason to notice you, they won't. People are too wrapped up in their own shit to care."

"Even teachers?"

My vision got foggy and my head jerked to the side, like I was checking over my shoulder. But there was nothing there but a wall.

"Yeah," I finally said. "If you blend into the middle of the class, not as bright as the achievers but not as dumb as the washouts and drama queens, teachers leave you alone too."

I rubbed my eyes. My throat was suddenly sore, and my head felt heavy, like it might tip off my neck if I wasn't careful.

"Let's stop for now," Luis said, and I was glad he did.

**

Entry 3

So what if I don't have any friends IRL. I don't need them. I get all the interaction I need on WoW. I can have just as many pointless conversations about stupid shit online, I don't need to have all the awkwardness that goes along with FtF BS.

I bet Luis thinks I'm a loser, but I know better. I don't really care what he thinks anyway.

**

"YOU LOOK LIKE YOU'RE FEELING A LITTLE BETTER."

I nodded. "I just get sleepy real easy."

"Do you dream?"

I snorted. "Not that I can remember, Dr. Freud."

He smiled. "Well, sometimes our subconscious tries to lend a hand in recovering memory. You should write down anything you dream right away, it may really help."

"Okay." But there was nothing to write.

"So, picking up from last time: it sounds to me like you were the kind of student who treated the school day as something to be survived. Get in, get out, go home, get the hell away from there. Sound right?"

I smiled. "You got it."

"So you weren't the sort to go to school events, football games, pep rallies, et cetera."

I shook my head. "Always sounded tedious to me."

"What about prom? More tedium?"

"I wasn't interested in adding to the teen mother population. It's already such a drain on the system."

He laughed. "What about girls?"

"What about them?"

"Were you ever interested?"

"In giggly manipulators that care more about how they look than how anyone around them feels? Not especially."

"Oh, come on. They're not all like that."

"Yeah, that's true. I just..."

I hadn't thought about Gracie in a long time. She definitely wasn't a giggly backstabber. I wondered where she was at that moment. Probably at work at the coffee shop, wearing her green apron.

Luis was looking at me. "Just what?"

"Huh? Oh. I just never got the point."

"The point of girls?"

"The point of going out with them. Of creating bullshit teenage drama when we're all just going to move on with life anyway. None of it lasts, so why bother?"

"Well, what about sex? That's a common motivator for young men when it comes to dating."

I shrugged.

"Are you attracted to women?"

"I'm not gay."

"I didn't ask that. Some people just don't feel the strong hormonal pull that happens to the majority of young men at your age."

"I'm not asexual," I said. "I like a nice set of tits as much as the next guy. I just..."

"If this is making you uncomfortable we can talk about something else."

"No, it's okay. I just knew pretty quickly that it wasn't in the cards for me. So why bother?"

"What wasn't in the cards?"

"Being good with girls. I know my zits are there, I know I'm awkward as hell whenever I'm around them. I wouldn't know the first thing to say, so I never did."

"Do you feel like you missed out?"

I thought about Gracie again, and that stabbing feeling I got in my gut whenever I saw her with that dick Craig. But hey, if she wanted to be stupid and hang out with a total asshole, what business of it was mine?

"Not really," I said. "I'd see so many arguments and tears and just total bullshit in these so-called relationships. Why? So they could fuck? Shit, I'd rather jerk off and save myself the drama."

He laughed. "It can be a pretty ridiculous dance. But didn't any of your classmates seem happy? Like they were enjoying it?"

I remembered Connor and Steph, how she would touch his arm, he would squeeze her hand, and they'd laugh. Everything seemed so easy with them, they never stuttered, or had those awkward-as-hell pauses, they were just two people comfortable with each other.

I remembered watching them in the hall and thinking that would never be my life, that I'd never have that kind of happiness. Like joy was a sturdy house with a roaring fire in the hearth, and that the rest of my days would be spent outside in the wind and cold.

"Yeah," I said. "Sometimes it looked like fun."

**

Entry 4

I'm climbing a ladder along a locker wall at my high school. There's hundreds all in a row, everyone has their own. Connor and Steph are climbing beside me, laughing and joking as they go. They don't notice me, of course.

Soon they find a knob along the locker wall, and when they turn it, it's not a locker door but a huge front door to a house.

They embrace and slip inside. I can feel the warmth for a quick second before they close the door behind them.

I keep climbing. The rungs are cool in my grip. I see Gracie in the distance, climbing with a focused look on her face. I call and wave, but she doesn't see me.

The rungs get farther apart, so I have to haul myself over one and straddle it. And then I can't reach the next one. It's cold and fog is rolling in.

I stand as straight as possible, bend my knees, and jump as far out as I can.

I'm falling and falling. I try to scream but nothing comes out.

**

"HOW'S YOUR HOME LIFE? YOU GET ALONG WITH YOUR mom?"

"Sure."

"Does she work?"

"Yeah. Swing shifts at the hospital."

"Swing shifts? So, I imagine you don't see each other very much."

"Yup. That's why we get along."

"I see. She hassle you?"

I shook my head. "She's just kinda checked out."

"What does that mean?"

"Well, when my supposed father died a few years back, her give-a-fuck factor fell off big time. She holds her job okay, but she doesn't do much else. Besides drink."

"She ever get nasty with you?"

"Nope. She just hits the bottle and goes online. Fuck if I know what she does on her computer. But she leaves me alone, so I don't mind."

"Does her drinking get in the way of cooking or minding the house?"

"My mom hasn't cooked me a meal or cleaned the house in three years."

That stopped him. His jaw hung open for a moment. "Really?"

I nodded. "I feed myself and I keep my room and bathroom clean. The rest is her issue."

"But she's not really being your mother, is she? It sounds more like she's a problem roommate."

"There's no problem."

He blinked. "Does she get the bills paid?"

"Most of the time. I keep track of them, and once in a while I have to pay the water bill or the internet because she forgets. But she barely ever misses work."

"I bet you can't wait to get out of there."

I shrugged. "It's not so bad."

Luis's eyes widened. "Not so bad? Your home is a mess, so you can't bring friends over, much less a girl. And you're having to feed yourself, pay bills? You may as well live on your own, not worry about your mother's drama."

"There's no drama," I said. "I told you, she leaves me alone. And I can't afford rent."

"You could once you got a full-time job."

"I guess, but..."

"But?"

"Then who'd take care of her?"

He stared at me.

I shrugged. "She's my mom, I can't just abandon her."

He sighed. "You're not her parent, Devin. She's yours."

"Maybe once," I said. "I can't remember that anymore."

**

Entry 5

I don't feel so great.

My stomach is hurting more. Not so much the nausea and puking, more of a steady, building ache. They drug me up with painkillers but they wear off. Dr. Pearsall doesn't seem alarmed.

Her calmness is reassuring, but I wish she'd tell me what's going on. She just tells me to discuss it with my counselor. But all Luis wants to talk about is my life.

I don't know who's going to pay for all this. I've been here three days already.

**

8/7 15:35

Patient "Devin" presents with stomach pain, restlessness, agitation. Percoset effective, but requiring larger and larger doses.

Serum administration scheduled for tomorrow. Have discussed urgency with Luis, who assured me progress is being made and a breakthrough is near.

Sedation is an option, and the Tranquility Team is standing by for when the serum is applied.

-T. Pearsall

**

"I STILL CAN'T REMEMBER SHIT," I SAID. "AND I DON'T SEE how talking about my life is helping me."

"It's helping me," Luis said. "Actually it's helped a great deal."

"Well, good for you!" I said, raising my hands in mock celebration. "How about for me, the guy that supposedly showed up here covered in blood?"

"I know a lot more about your situation now," he said calmly. "And so I have a pretty good idea of what happened."

"You do? Then tell me!"

"You need to remember on your own. I'm going to lead you there."

"Fine," I said. "What do you want to talk about now? My best Minesweeper score? How about my favorite movie? It's 'The Salton Sea,' by the way, a real underrated modern noir."

"I want to talk about school some more," he said. I rolled my eyes. "Bear with me. You're a smart guy, I bet you could do really well if you wanted to. What was your favorite subject?"

"I liked literature," I said. "I like reading, and seeing how an author will do stuff between the lines."

"Were you good at it?"

I nodded. "It seemed pretty easy to me. And I really liked it, so it wasn't work. It was fun."

He smiled. "Did your talent attract the attention of your teacher?"

My vision got blurry again, and the muscles in my right arm twitched. Monica. I could clearly see her bright blue eyes, the smooth, flawless skin of her face. The small smile full of mystery and danger.

"Yeah, actually," I said, remembering. "I wrote a paper about 'Edgar Huntly' that Monica - Ms. Lefave - really liked. She said I opened her mind to early American gothic literature in a completely new way. She even invited me over to her house to discuss it."

"Really? Did you go?"

"Yeah, the next night." My right arm began to tingle, and my heart was pounding. "I'd forgotten all about it until now." But when I tried to think about that visit I saw the gray cloud again.

"You're frowning," Luis said.

"Yeah," I said slowly. "I'm having a hard time remembering what happened." My mouth was dry and I had a strange, acidic taste on my tongue.

"How long ago was it?"

"Not too long. Maybe a month before graduation." I tried to think about Monica, but every time I thought of her face, the picture in my mind clouded up and she vanished.

"Well, let's start with the basics. Was it day or night when you went?"

"Evening. The street lights were just coming on."

"Do you remember what her house looked like?"

I nodded. "It was in a nicer neighborhood at the end of a cul-de-sac. Nothing too fancy. I remember a big covered porch with a bench."

"Okay. Do you remember how you felt as you walked to her door? Were you nervous?"

"Actually I was pretty relaxed," I remembered, surprising myself. "It was a chance to talk about literature without all the distractions of high school. I mean, I didn't want to disappoint her, but I felt like I knew my stuff. That's right - I remember studying the day before I went over so I'd have some examples fresh in my mind."

He nodded. "Do you remember what Ms. Lefave looked like that night?"

The cloud still obscured her features, so I shrugged.

"All right. What did you do when you went inside? Did you have dinner?"

My heart was really pounding now and my throat felt tight. "Um. She had this, like, sitting room, with nice leather couches and a fireplace. We started talking, and..."

"And? What did you talk about?"

I swallowed hard. I started shaking really bad and a shimmering purple cloud blotched out Luis's face and quickly spread toward the corners of my vision. "I don't feel so-" was what I squeaked out before everything went black.

**

8/7 20:15

Patient "Devin" presents with catatonia
and lethargy, expected symptoms given
Counselor Luis's report. In same report
Luis recommends delay of Serum
administration as he believes important
memories are close at hand. Protocol
dictates Serum administration as soon as
traumatic memory recall produces the
pseudo-psychotic break, but Luis assures
me that this case is exceptional.

I trust Luis's judgment but am insisting
on intensive monitoring. Nurse will be
just outside door on every session until
Serum is administered. In the meantime
prescribing Klonopin/Xanax cocktail to
produce semi-conscious sedation.

                                    -T. Pearsall

**

Entry 6

Really loopy now. Not much pain. Comfortably numb like that
song. Actually more like not-uncomfortably numb.

How did I forget about Monica until yesterday? And why is it
so hard to think about her now? That gray cloud gets in the
way, and then the most random thing will distract me. Right
now it's trying to remember the password on my computer.
Which is pretty stupid seeing as how I can't get to it.

I don't even know what I'd do if I could. But I really want to see if I'm right. For some reason.

I heard that the brain tries to protect itself by making the memories of bad shit hard to get to. Which means that whatever went down that got me here probably involved Monica.

That would suck. She was very cool to me.

From what I can remember, anyway.

**

"CAN'T YOU JUST TELL ME WHAT HAPPENED? I MEAN, THIS is obviously tough on me."

"I never said I knew what happened," Luis said. "I said I have a pretty good idea. But even if I did know, it's really important that you remember on your own. Take it from me, it's way worse to try to mold your memories around what someone tells you happened. You end up second-guessing yourself for years."

I sighed. My head felt like a balloon that would float away if it wasn't attached to my neck. "Whatever. If you say so."

"I do. Okay. So let's go back to that visit to Ms. Lefave's house. I actually think you're in a state where the memories will be easier to produce."

"I won't pass out?"

"I don't think so. Not saying it'll be a picnic either."

"Okay." I took a deep breath. I really did want to know what happened. It was a strange feeling to have a hole in my memory. It made me really curious and, given where I was, pretty damn worried. "Where'd I leave off?"

"You were in Ms. Lefave's sitting room, and I asked what you talked about."

I concentrated. I could see myself in that room, could feel the cool leather under my legs. She sat in a chair to my left. "She looked good," I said. "She wore a black skirt to her knees and a deep red blouse, you know the kind that are all bunched up along the top so like you can tell there are some great tits there but it's not like, obvious? She always looked so classy, like she knew she was hot but she didn't need to show it off.

"And her hair looked great, wavy black resting on her shoulders, and her bright blue eyes were looking at me, like she was really interested in what I had to say, and I'm staring, you know? I'm trying not to, but I'm really distracted by how pretty she is and I'm thinking, come on Devin, keep it together, show her you're not some ordinary stupid teenage dude, and I'm stuttering, and my heart's in my throat, and I start sweating even though her place is nice and cool, and nothing I say makes any sense, and I start apologizing, and she waves her hand and smiles, says it's okay, that she knows what the problem is."

I stopped. The gray cloud was in that sitting room with me, but it was like a strong breeze came up now and again and made the cloud see-through. I didn't know what was bringing on that wind but I tried not to dwell too much on anything just in case the wind stopped and made all my memories cloudy again.

"So before I know it," I continued, "she's on her knees in front of me and her hands are on my thighs. I was too stunned to say anything, and she says it's all right, she'll take care of it. And then she's undoing my pants and touching me and I figure I must be dreaming or something. And then I'm there, you know, and she puts her mouth on me, and as I'm looking, trying not to have a fucking heart attack, she looks at me, and that was it, it was all over, if you know what I mean.

"And my brain is exploding, and I see a bunch of stars, and she's massaging me, telling me it's all right, that I did real good, and then I catch my breath, and she smiles again, and I'm wondering what the fuck just happened. She excuses herself, gets up and leaves the room, and I sit there like a truck just hit me.

"I zip up, and I think, did that just happen? Did she just up and do that? And I just sit there, I don't know what else to do, and just when my shoulders start to relax a little she walks back in and asks if I feel better.

"I don't know what the fuck to say to that, but I nod, and she says good, now with that out of the way, we can really talk. And that's that we did. We talked about literature for like two hours."

I shook my head. "And the whole time I'm thinking, she's treating it like no big deal, so I should do the same, she'd be disappointed if I did anything else. So, impossible as it was, I tried not to think about it the rest of the night. And she never says a thing about it. Like it meant nothing at all."

I stared into space for a while. I remembered thinking that maybe that's what sophisticated people thought about sex, like it's some biological nuisance to be handled and forgotten. It really meant nothing to her.

"Here you go," Luis said. He held a tissue in his hand and was offering it to me. I didn't know why at first, but after a second I felt the tears on my cheeks, the snot running over my lip. I wondered how long I'd been crying.

I felt like I should've been embarrassed, sitting there crying in front of him, but I wasn't. Maybe it was the drugs.

"Was that your first sexual experience?" he asked.

I nodded. That part was kind of embarrassing. "Can we stop for now? I'm kind of exhausted."

"Okay." He leaned forward. "I want you to remember this, Devin: it was wrong of her to do that to you. I don't care if you were eighteen at the time. She took advantage of you and that wasn't right."

I shrugged. "I didn't tell her to stop."

"She put you in an impossible position. There's no way any young man in your situation could've behaved any differently. And even if you had said something, she wouldn't have stopped."

"Okay," I said.

I wasn't really listening. All I wanted to do is lie down in my hospital bed and curl up into a ball for a few months.

**

Entry 7

I remember that night, lying awake, staring at the ceiling. I thought about all the news reports I'd seen on TV, the scandals of teachers seducing students, and how much more publicity the story got if it was a woman teacher. I remember a follow-up article I'd read about how, contrary to locker-room belief, the so-called 'abuse' is actually really damaging to the young men involved. Trust issues, attachment problems, and so on. There was even a TV courtroom drama showing the dude getting all head-over-heels for his not-that-hot teacher.

That wasn't going to be me. I wasn't going to get obsessed.

Because that would disappoint her. It'd be weak. And I was going to be strong for her.

Shit, what did I do?

Did I get jealous and kill her?

I don't have violence in me, let alone murder.

But something did happen. That's for damn sure.

**

"THE NEXT FEW DAYS I WALKED ON AIR. I LOOKED around at all the other guys in class and knew none of them could say what I could. None of them had what I had, even if nothing else ever happened and all I ended up with were memories.

"And I did great at not giving anything away. I never acted giddy, never stared at her, never even talked to her, because that would've been different. No, I stayed to my normal invisible routine.

"And so did Monica. She never gave me a second glance, never said anything that would've been out of the ordinary for a classroom. But when she smiled at me, it was like electric shocks hitting my chest."

I remembered sitting in class, invisible in the back as always, pretending to read "The Old Man and the Sea" but actually thinking about Monica, about how happy I was making her by staying silent and acting normal. No one would ever know, but that was fine by me. I didn't care what anyone thought.

I think Gracie tried to talk to me during that time, but I was even more distant and strange than normal. I swallowed hard. What if she was interested in me then? I probably wouldn't have cared.

"What happened next?" Luis asked.

"Like a week later I got a text message. It said 'It's Monica. I've got a surprise for you.' And I thought it was stupid, that's how the cops connect you to people, they check your phone logs, but then I thought, she's smarter than that, this is probably a pre-paid throw-away phone.

"So I text back, 'What's that?' and she says, 'Come to my house midnight graduation night. Be discreet.' I say 'I will. Is it a graduation gift?' She says, 'It's a surprise. Don't text me again.' So I didn't."

"How long was it till graduation?"

"Another two and a half weeks."

"I bet those were some long days."

"That's the truth," I said. "But I took it like it was a mission, or a test. In the end Monica would be so happy with my discipline, with my strength. There was no way I would ruin it for her. Or myself."

"Did you go to graduation?"

"Nah."

Luis's eyebrows arched. "Really? That's a big thing, graduating from high school. Sort of a passage from one stage of life into the next."

I shrugged. "My mother said she couldn't get the night off. And it wasn't like I was going to celebrate with a bunch of friends."

"I see. So what did you do that night?"

"Paced around my room like a total nervous wreck."

"Are you nervous right now?"

I shrugged. "Not really."

He pointed at my hands. "Your knuckles are white."

I looked down. I was gripping the bottom of the chair with both hands and yes, my knuckles were white. "Oh. Well, I am kind of nervous. I'm afraid I did something to her."

"Don't judge yourself yet," Luis said. "Let's see what you remember first."

"THERE WASN'T A MR. LEFAVE, RIGHT?"

I shook my head. "Monica never wore a ring, never mentioned anyone else, and I didn't see any evidence of a dude living at her house."

"Okay. So take me to that night."

I took a deep breath. "I dressed kind of nice, slacks and a button-up shirt. I brushed my teeth like four times after 11 o'clock.

"I knock on her door, and she opens it, and she's wearing this black dress, really simple but she's just as hot as all hell, and her eyes are so intense it's like they're glowing electric blue. She just says, 'Come in.' My heart's in my throat so all I say is 'Hi.'

"She tells me to follow her, and we go down this dark hallway and into this huge bedroom. Everything in there is red, because the light is red, and I can't tell where it's coming from. 'Sit down on the bed,' she says, and I do, and it's all slick and satiny, and my heart's pounding.

"'Are you ready for your surprise?' she says. And her skin, her face, her eyes are all red in this light, but she's smiling at me, and all I can say is 'sure.'

"And then she lifts one shoulder, her red eyes locked on me the whole time, and lifts another, and then that dress drops to the ground. And she wasn't wearing anything else.

"So she's naked, and my heart's pounding even harder, and she says, 'Surprise.'"

My throat locked up, and I coughed a few times. My breath was coming really shallow and I had to inhale slowly a few times.

"And then you had sex?" Luis offered.

I nodded. "It was over really quickly. I was so worried about being finished too soon or not doing something right that the end wasn't all that great."

"What did she say about it?"

"Nothing," I said. "She just laughed, touched my cheek and said, 'you're so cute.' So I mean, on one hand, I felt great, I just had sex with a really hot, amazing woman, but on the other, I felt like shit, because I couldn't tell if I did that great. We never even kissed.

"But one thing was for sure: I was exhausted. So I just kinda lay there on the bed, and she says, 'you just relax,' so I do."

And then that big gray cloud, which had been absent since my story started, parked itself in that red room with me.

"What happened next, Devin?"

I waited for the cloud to dissipate in my memory, but it didn't. I had sex with her, it felt great and really shitty at the same time, and...

"Did you fall asleep?"

"I think so," I said slowly. "I was really tired after all that adrenalin wore off."

"Did you have a dream?"

At the word 'dream', an image flashed into my mind: Monica, in that black dress, her face and eyes red, long fangs protruding from her open mouth.

And then the image disappeared into the cloud, like a candle flame snuffed to smoke.

"Yeah," I said. "Monica was a monster, with these glowing red eyes and huge fangs. That's weird."

"Uh-huh," Luis said. "Tell me what you felt when you woke up, Devin."

I closed my eyes and concentrated. The gray cloud didn't budge, but I could hear something: laughter. Monica's laughter.

And pain.

Pain shooting through my chest, up to my neck, like a lightning bolt.

"What are you feeling, Devin?"

"Pain," I gasped. I could still feel the barbs tearing through my veins. "And I can hear her laughing."

"All right," Luis said. "What else?"

"I can't move," I remembered. "I'm so tired, but I can't even roll over." I opened my eyes. "Did she drug me?"

"We didn't find any drugs in your system," he said. "What happened next? Find the memory, Devin. It's waiting for you."

I closed my eyes again. Tired, pain, Monica's laughter. "Eventually I just want to be away from her," I said.

"Did you say that to Ms. Lefave?"

And then I was in the red room, and I remembered mumbling, "I'm tired, I'm gonna go home," and she laughed, and she said, "This is home now." And I didn't get it, and when my frown showed my confusion, she just laughed harder. "You'll soon see," she said.

And then I was sleepy again, and when I woke up she wasn't there. I got up and my head was spinning, I had to steady myself for what felt like forever just to stand up. It was dim in there, but my toes kicked my pants on the floor, so I scooped them up. I wandered toward where I thought the door was, but when I opened it I found a bathroom. Which was actually pretty fortunate because I realized I had to pee really bad.

So I took a piss, steadying my hand on the wall so I didn't sprinkle the floor, and when I was done I started to pull my pants on, and I got a twinge in my neck.

It ached really bad, especially when I turned my head to the side. The skin felt sticky, and I wanted to check it out in the mirror but I couldn't find one in the room. Which seemed really weird to me, what chick doesn't have a mirror in her bathroom?

But then I noticed the polished chrome of the shower door frame, and I stepped up to take a look...

"Devin? Can you hear me?"

The cloud was right between my eyes and the chrome. My neck hurt really bad, I was swaying...

"Where are you now, Devin?"

My chest was suddenly cold and my hands were shaking. I wanted to turn away from the chrome reflection, but I couldn't, I had to see what happened...

"I'm in the bathroom," I mumbled. "My neck hurts really bad and the skin is sticky, but I can't find a mirror to see what's going on. There's some chrome on the frame of the shower door, but..."

"But what?"

"I can't... I can't remember what I see."

"Can't or won't?"

I shivered. "I think I'm afraid of what's there."

"You're in a safe place now," Luis said. "You're going to be okay. But that memory is going to unlock something, something very important. Our course of action, of healing, will be determined by what you see in that reflection. But I can't see it for you. You have to see it for yourself."

I ground my teeth. I did want to know what happened. But my body was telling me not to find out.

I closed my eyes and concentrated on the gray cloud. In a safe place.

I need the truth.

The cloud dissipated.

TWO BLACK HOLES IN THE REFLECTION, WITH A TRAIL OF dried blood snaking down my neck.

"This is home now..."

That was why there was no mirror in the bathroom.

"You'll soon see..."

I heard her laughter again; I spun behind me, but there was no one there.

I dashed back into the bedroom, pulled aside the first set of heavy drapes I found, and found two thick boards where the window should be.

My heart was in my throat. It couldn't be. Monica was a teacher at the high school!

But had I ever seen her in the sun?

The school was close to downtown, it had an underground parking garage.

"What are you thinking, Devin?"

"Vampire," I said. My hand was on my neck and the rest of me was shivering. I swallowed hard. "I thought Monica was a vampire. I went nuts, huh."

"Why did you think she was a vampire?" he said, his tone a little too matter-of-fact.

I sighed. "There were two black bite marks on my neck and dried blood running from them. There were no mirrors or windows in the room, and I couldn't remember ever seeing her in the sun."

"So what did you do next?"

It all came back to me now. "I threw a chair into the boards where the window should've been, for some reason thinking that was the only way out of the room. It didn't do anything but splinter the wood a little, but that gave me an idea.

"I pried a chunk of wood from the board, then found my cell phone in my pants pocket. It told me it was two in the afternoon; if Monica was a vampire, then she'd be sleeping.

"I found the door back to the hallway and started to search the house as quietly as I could. I found a stairwell going down to some kind of root cellar. I used my cell phone as a flashlight, and there she was, lying in a groove dug out of the earth. She was still wearing that black dress.

"And I did what I had to."

"What'd you do, Devin?"

"I staked the bitch," I said. "It wasn't as easy as I thought it would be, my first strike didn't go in very far. And then she woke up, looked at me her eyes all cloudy, mumbled something and laughed. I tried again, and this time it was like I hit an artery or something because blood fountained up and sprayed me in the face. Then she was screaming, scratching at me, but I kept jabbing, over and over again, until she stopped fighting."

I shook my head. "So I guess I'm going to prison now. I guess it's the right place for me. Never thought I could do something like that."

I held my head in my hands. I killed someone. No wonder both my body and mind were working so hard to prevent me from remembering. I was a murderer. And here I'd just confessed. Why didn't I ask for a lawyer or something? Luis railroaded me into spilling it all out with his cockamamie talk of 'healing.'

I sighed. I couldn't be mad. I would get what I deserved, and that was a good thing. I obviously was a danger to myself and others and needed a great deal of psychiatric help.

"I'm glad it all came back to you," Luis said, leaning forward. "Now the real healing can begin."

And he smiled.

I JUST STARED AT HIM. HOW COULD HE BE SMILING? DID he get off on murder confessions? What kind of sick bastard was I dealing with, anyway?

He stood up and moved to his desk. "I'm going to show you something," he said as he opened a drawer, "that may change how you feel about the situation right now."

Luis pulled out a manila folder, came back to his chair and sat down. "This is a picture taken at Ms. Lefave's residence soon after you were picked up."

He handed me the folder. Inside it was a glossy photo of Monica's root cellar, brightly lit. I recognized the groove of earth where she lay when I killed her.

Where her body should have been was an evenly distributed pile of gray ash, like someone had dumped the contents of a charcoal barbecue into the groove and then smoothed out the mound.

"I don't get it," I said. "Was there a fire?"

"Nope," Luis said. "That's just what happens after you stake a vampire."

I blinked. "Real funny," I eventually said.

"No joke," he said. "Your Ms. Lefave was a vampire. We'd been searching for her for a few months. We thought she'd moved to this area but we hadn't thought to check the high schools. It's a pretty elaborate cover, the first we've seen-"

"She really was a vampire," I said, incredulous.

"Yeah," Luis said, rubbing his hands on his pants. "A bad one. We think she killed a dozen people in the metro area. You know, you've done something really remarkable."

"Huh?" Vampires were real? My vision of her with the fangs wasn't a dream?

"Victims almost never kill vamps," Luis said. "The physical and emotional control is far too great. Victims will defend and protect their vampire, sometimes even sacrifice themselves for their sake. We call it enthrallment, kind of a cross between love, obsession and brainwashing.

"What you did was really amazing," Luis continued. "It took some serious strength and courage."

I just stared at him. "This isn't a joke," I said.

He shook his head. "I should probably tell you where you are now."

"WE'RE NOT A HOSPITAL," HE SAID, "THOUGH WE DO HAVE a wing with an infirmary and a couple of rooms. What we are is the Orphanage, a shelter for victims of vampires. We seek out vamps, kill them and rehabilitate their living victims. And that's what you are, Devin."

A cool, clean feeling blossomed in my chest. I wasn't crazy, and I wasn't a criminal. I didn't like the word 'victim' but it sounded way better than 'murderer.' "Is that why I was so sick?"

Luis's expression darkened. "You still are sick," he said. "And there's something you need to realize." He looked down for a moment, rubbed his fingers together, then looked back at me. "At some point - we're thinking when you staked her - you were exposed to Ms. Lefave's blood. It got into the wound on your neck."

I touched my neck, remembering it from the chrome reflection in the bathroom. But there was nothing there but smooth skin.

"You don't feel it because the infected blood healed the wound. But that blood - and the infection - is inside you now."

I squinted. "Infection?" My vision went white and my hands gripped the sides of my head. "Oh god, are you saying I'm a vampire now?"

"No," he said. "But if your condition was left untreated, you would become one."

My heart was pounding. "So - so what does it mean? Is there a cure?"

"No," Luis said. "But we can slow the infection to a crawl. It takes treatment and discipline, but it's a condition you can live with."

My hands moved to the bottom of the chair and I held on, afraid I was going to fall off. "You said slow, not stop," I said. "How long..."

"I've had it for sixteen years," Luis said. "If you're careful about the sun and never give into your blood cravings, you can live a long time with this condition.

"We call ourselves Orphans," he said. "We've turned away from our parent, who made us like this. Or, like in your case," he said with a smile, "we staked their asses."

**

Entry 8

So now I'm an Orphan. It's strange, I don't really feel different, but they say the 'serum' they gave me keeps the symptoms at bay for a while. But, slowly, I'll start thinking about blood, hearing it push through people's veins, smelling it like a shark or a lion does. It'll get so distracting that I could literally go nuts thinking about it. And if I ever satisfy the craving, I'll just think about it more, need it more, and then I'm a vampire and the Orphans will stick a stake in my chest.

They say I can take sunlight, but not much. Two minutes will bring a burn. Ten minutes will make me start puking and twenty will kill me. I guess that's not so bad, I wasn't really an outdoor person as it was.

My whole life has changed. But I don't really miss the old one.

The Orphanage is my home now. My fellow Orphans here are really cool. They don't mind explaining anything, or telling their own stories about vampires that totally fucked them over. And they really respect what I did. Most of them had their vamps killed by other Orphans on the hunt. They tell me they still think about their vamps, miss them in a sick way, even though they're dead. It's something they deal with every day.

As for me... I dunno. I can't help but think about Monica whenever I think about my infection. Luis says the true test will be when I start my next relationship, how much I think about her then. He's optimistic, though, seeing as how I "staked her ass."

Who knows when I'll be ready for a relationship. Luis says they encourage them here, because going through this alone is impossible.

One thing I know I'm ready for is to hunt vampires. I keep picturing Gracie walking to her car after her shift with some dude stalking her, tricking her, deceiving her...

I've got to protect her, any way that I can. Yeah, I have to keep a secret, but that's nothing new for me.

My mom never saw me during daylight hours anyway, so keeping all this from her will be easy. I'll just tell her I found my own place. I'll visit her at work and watch the bills from online. I couldn't stay with her forever, I guess.

It's such a complete change, sometimes I think "why me?" But every time I get those thoughts I remember something Luis said: it happened to me because I was an easy target. That's how vampires operate. They find the most vulnerable, enthrall them, use them, drink them, kill them.

It's funny. I'm in danger of turning into a vampire, and I'll have to live with this terrible infection for the rest of my (probably short) life. But I'm happier now than I can ever remember.

I've got friends, respect, direction. Never really had any of those before. And now I know I'm capable of "some serious strength and courage."

It doesn't seem right, but I find myself feeling grateful to Monica. It doesn't really matter if she was a horrible, evil beast that manipulated and abused me. She gave my life purpose, and I'll be indebted to her forever for that.

Looks like I'm going to need a lot more therapy.

The DanneR Party

Entry 1: 10/2/07, 4:20pm

Today I'm Feeling: lonely, but adventurous

After ten solid minutes of thought, I decided to give my online friends a look into my messed-up life. I think it'll be fun. Plus my contact info changes so much from year to year that some of the cool people I've met online have a hard time finding me. Big thanks to Uncle PJ for helping me get moving with the web-stuff.

But I've got to be careful here. I'm going to have to be vague (or l33t) so my dad doesn't find this on some random google search. Cuz I know he'd try. He's so paranoid. I've got to scrub the browser histories after every entry. That's not a problem, though. I've got a neat little app that does it with just a double click and a smile. And I've got dirt on Uncle PJ. He'll be good. ;)

Anyway, if my dad found out that I was broadcasting my thoughts to the ether he'd totally freak out and lock me out of the computer again. And there's no way I'm gonna use the computers at school, I don't have the time. So I'm gonna use nicknames for my friends, school, town, etc. But hopefully the face of my true thoughts will show through my veil of lies. I guess that's what I hope about every part of my life.

I'll try to update it every day, but I can't make any promises. Just like every other part of my life.

See you next time,
DanneR

Song Stuck In My Head: "Lips Like Sugar", Echo & the Bunnymen

**

Entry 2: 10/3/07, 7:50pm

Today I'm Feeling: bored, as usual

School was pointless as usual, though Deni and I met a cool new girl at lunch. Her name is Melissa and she's got bright pink hair and an eyebrow ring. She's a little spazzy, but she's very friendly, and she liked my Doc Martens. We'll see how it goes. Our weirdo lunch table has seen new transfers before, only to have them bail after their first week. Like Adrian, that ass.

I think Mom is getting sick again. She was spacier than usual when she drove me home from school. I told her she ought to see a doctor, but I know she'll just wait till my Aunt visits us next week.

That brings me to the beginning of my running list!:

WEIRD THINGS ABOUT MY FAMILY:

#1) None of us has seen a doctor or gone to a hospital for as long as I can remember.

My parents have a bunch of reasons – too expensive, you just get sicker around all those sick people, your DNA gets sent to a big database in the Pentagon, etc. I think Aunt T@mmi3 is a physician's assistant or something, and she takes good care of us. But I've never met anybody else who has their own doctor who makes house calls monthly.

And my rents are serious about me not going to the hospital. I remember one time, four or five moves ago, I fell off my bike and banged my elbow so hard that it wouldn't straighten. But my rents just called Aunt T@mmi3, who put my arm in a sling and told me to be more careful.

My arm's fine, so I guess I can't really complain. But it's still weird.

Getting tired,
DanneR

Song Stuck In My Head: "Doctor", Lusk

**

Entry #3: 10/4/07, 10:00pm

Today I'm Feeling: imprisoned

Hey again. Another dull day, but I think Melissa likes us. Which is cool, because I think I like her. She asked if I wanted to go get coffee tonight, but of course I can't, because I'm not allowed to leave the house on school nights. So instead I'm here, casting my futile thoughts into the vast emptiness. How appropriate.

If you know me, you know my parents are very strict. I can't go out on school nights, and whenever I am somewhere without them I have to call to check in every hour. If I don't check in, they call me: the number of rings it takes me to answer is how many weeks I'm grounded. If I don't answer, they come looking for me. I don't know what my punishment would be then. Maybe they'd break my fingers. Or chain me in the basement.

I guess it could be worse. At least I don't have to do a bunch of extracurricular crap at school. But then we move around so much, there wouldn't be much point.

Ugh, I really hope we don't move again soon. I would hate to have to start over at a new high school. Plus I really like this area. It's very green here, and the ocean isn't far away. (Was that vague enough? There's only what, 2,000 miles of coastline in the US and Canada?)

Maybe I'll invite Deni and Melissa over here. The rents are usually pretty cool about that. They just want me in sight, I guess. It might be tough to find a night when Mom is in town and Dad's not at work, though. Maybe next week.

More ramblings to come...

Song stuck in my head: "There's More To Life Than This", Bjork

**

Entry #4: 10/6/07, 7:20pm

Today I'm Feeling: sleepy

Weird, disturbing dreams last night. I don't remember much other than trying to get the bear chasing me to go after my horse instead of me, which made me feel really guilty.

I was a zombie through most of school, and didn't notice until after Painting that Adrian was really nice to me all throughout the period. He said he liked my abstract project and asked if I was feeling okay. He even gave me his Mountain Dew (unopened). I wonder what he's up to...

I hope this bout of insomnia doesn't last. Dad says I inherited his nocturnal leanings. He works from 10pm to 6am at a water treatment plant, and he says it'd be hell for him if he had to do any real thinking at 8:30am. Oh well, only one more year of high school after this to go...

DanneR

Song Stuck In My Head: "Sleep," Conjure One

**

Entry #5: 10/7/07, 10:04pm

Today I'm Feeling: paralyzed

So it's Friday, but I spent most of the day in bed because I have no energy. I keep drifting in and out of dreams (fantasies? delusions?), each one more depressing than the last.

The last one I remember I was on my back, floating down a slow-moving river, and beautiful, tragic, eyeless angels skittered above me in a starry night sky, gesturing upriver, the opposite way I was moving. Their mouths moved, but I couldn't hear anything they said. Still, I understood that they were urging me to get out of the river, that the current was leading me to something terrible. But I couldn't move my arms or legs. I was lucky I wasn't drowning. The river was going to take me where it would, and there was nothing I could do about it.

I get sick like this every now and then, and if it lasts more than a day, Mom lays hands on me and prays to her goddess...

WEIRD THINGS ABOUT MY FAMILY:

#2) My parents believe in some weird pagan fire goddess, whose name I'm not going to write, but from now on I'll call 'Z'. They say that Z is the reason we're alive, that She 'watches out for us,' 'guides us to serenity,' and 'delivers us from self-destruction.'

My mom is a lot more devout than my dad. She's always creating the symbol of Z, which is an h0urg1a55 bathed in flame. The basement is filled with Mom's paintings, sketches, sculptures, even pottery with Z's symbol all over it, and at least once a day she's down there meditating. She says that without Z she'd be 'lost,' and she's always trying to get me down there to pray with her. I remember doing it a lot when I was younger, but one day I said I'd rather go watch TV, and that was it. I'd never really felt anything anyway. Mom offers to pray with me every now and then, but she doesn't really push it.

My parents say it's important that I not tell anyone about their religious beliefs. They say that the world wouldn't understand, that we'd all be persecuted. They don't have anything to worry about – I'm not into telling anybody how weird my family is.

Well, except maybe the ether. But then, the ether understands me. It won't judge me.

Drifting away again...

DanneR

Song Stuck In My Head: "Pyramid Song", Radiohead

**

Entry #6: 10/8/07, 4:30pm

Today I'm Feeling: sick

Not much to say today. I'm a lot worse, my heart is thunking hard, and my gums are throbbing. I'm really thirsty, so I'm constantly drinking water and fruit juice, and so I'm always in the bathroom. My vision is blurring in time with my heartbeat and I have these shivering fits.

This happens to me around once a year. Aunt T@mmi3 gave me some good medicine last time, and Mom says she's on her way. In the meantime Mom wants me in the basement to 'pray for healing.' I'd rather take my chances with the nightmares in my own bed.

I hope Aunt T@mmi3's car doesn't break down.

DanneR

Song Stuck In My Head: "Shake The Disease", Hooverphonic

**

Entry #7: 10/9/07, 4:25pm

Today I'm Feeling: is delusion and whats real

whats real in my black glass black sands fallign meteors plunging fire into gravel btween my ears hering so mny voices babblign at once lanuages long forgotn blend together loud louder grind the dust to dust to ashess scattr wind blows harder & harder

spiders crawl out of me down my leg rip my black sand out of me aashess ashess we all fall down

we all fall down

we all fall down]

me gravel sand dust ashes air ether me

how I'd love to be a stone

**

Entry #8: 10/10/07, 7:11pm

Today I'm Feeling: better

What a difference a day makes. Aunt T@mmi3 came over yesterday while I was tripping (believe it or not, yesterday's post actually made perfect sense to me at the time.) She gave me some of that great medicine. I remember that it tasted like bubble gum and knocked me OUT!

I slept for 14 hours, and when I woke up I felt AMAZING. It's like I'm more alert, more energetic than ever before! The only bad part about this is that I had no excuse to miss school, which sucks. Figures I manage to get sick on the weekend.

I asked Aunt T@mmi3 what that medicine was, and why we don't just have it as part of a healthy breakfast. She said it's 1) expensive and 2) habit-forming. She wouldn't even tell me what it's called, so I wouldn't try to knock over a pharmacy to get more. I named it the "Last Resort," which sounds like a Twilight Zone episode. I can see a bellboy in a red uniform greeting me with "Good evening ma'am, and welcome to the Last Resort!"

Anyway it feels wonderful to not be sick any more. Deni was shocked to see me so smiley today. She kept asking me the name of the boy I'd met over the Internet, because why else would I be so giddy? No boy has ever made me feel like this, but if they can, I understand why so many girls my age are so boy-crazy.

I seriously can't remember feeling more alive than I have today. I feel like I could climb a mountain, or run a marathon, or swim across an ocean. Okay, maybe not an ocean, but possibly a sea, or maybe a large lake.

All right, I'm getting a little silly. Aunt T@mmi3's going to be staying with us for a while, partially to monitor me, and also because she's got business in the city. It's always cool when she stays with us, she's always got really good advice. She's more like an older sister than an aunt. And she's not really my aunt – she's not related to either of my parents – but that's what I've always called her. I hope we can hang out some time when the rents aren't around.

OK, if dad finds out that I've been logged in past one hour, he'll take my Internet away.

DanneR

Song Stuck In My Head: "I See Right Through To You", by DJ Encore

**

Entry #9: 10/12/07, 7:22pm

Today I'm Feeling: Riding High

Wow, another great day. I still feel fantastic, sleeping great, and I found out that I aced Monday's Geometry test – me? Ace a math test? Never!

I also made some good progress on my abstract painting, and I got Mom to agree to let Deni and Melissa come over tomorrow night because Aunt T@mmi3 is here to hover over us. Not that Aunt T@mmi3 will be a problem. She'll pretty much leave us alone if we want, but she'll probably make us some of her amazing chicken salad cups and generally be awesome.

I've got to clean my room!

DanneR

Song Stuck In My Head: "Rainy Days Never Stays", the brilliant green

**

Entry #10 : 10/13/07, 5:30pm

Today I'm Feeling: normal!

Last night was really great! Deni & Melissa came over around 7 – Melissa's got a car, that lucky s&*% – and neither of my weird parents were here to freak them out. Instead, Aunt T@mmi3 fussed over us as we watched a movie and hung out in my room. We saw 'A Series of Unfortunate Events', which was really cute. Deni says it's nothing like the books, but I liked it.

It made me wonder what it's like to have a sibling. Deni says having a younger half-sister isn't any fun, and Mel says having an older brother isn't as bad as it sounds. I guess I'll never know. Aunt T@mmi3 says Mom can't have any more children, that she was lucky to have me. I inherited that, by the way. Aunt T@mmi3 says that it's not impossible for me to have kids, but it would "take a series of miracles." I am utterly unbothered by that. At least I don't have to worry about birth control.

Anyway, Mel really likes Mom's style. She says she's never seen anything like our house – she says it's like we live in an art gallery, with all of Mom's sculptures & paintings and so few windows. Can't have the sunlight fading the artwork.

We talked about boys, and they grilled me on who I'd met. They just wouldn't believe that I'm just really happy to be healthy again! So...

I made someone up. His name is Daniel and he lives two states away. He likes cats and has a hearing impairment. I feel kinda bad about lying to my friends, but that's what they get for not believing me. In a week or so I'll tell them that 'Daniel' turned out to be gay. That ought to be fun.

Gotta go...

DanneR

Song Stuck In My Head: "Euphoria", by Delerium

**

Entry #11: 10/14/07, 9:30pm

Today I'm Feeling: Thank Gargamel It's Friday

I love Fridays. This one especially, because tomorrow I start a weekend where I'm healthy enough to enjoy it! I'm hoping to go to the mall with Deni & Mel, but we'll have to see what the rents say. Mom hasn't come home after leaving in a big hurry Wednesday night, and sometimes she's in a crappy mood when she gets back from her trips.

WEIRD THINGS ABOUT MY FAMILY:

#3) My mom is often gone for days at a time on short notice. She works for something called Et3rn41 H0p3 Ind\/5tri3s, and she's always traveling around the continent to see her 'clients'. From eavesdropping on her conversations with Dad, she apparently counsels addicts, but she absolutely refuses to talk about her work with me. I don't get why not. It's not like I'm a kid anymore. I know there's such things as junkies and alcoholics. Deni's scuzzy stepdad tried to sell me some pot once!

But as usual, my parents think I need to be protected from the realities of the big bad world out there, and so they're always extremely careful to not talk about Mom's work around me. It's such crap.

I'm the only girl I know whose mother will suddenly leave for days at a time. And then another 'Aunt' or 'Uncle' will suddenly show up and hang out at the house for a few days while Mom is gone. But that part I don't really mind. Whoever ends up visiting is usually way cooler than my parents. Except Uncle V. He's a weirdo.

But back to happier things. Adrian and I giggled all through Painting today. We passed this sketchpad back and forth, drawing the chatty freshman girls next door in Intro to Art so that they were missing limbs, or had their heads shoved up each others' asses. Mrs. K took the pad away from us, but I saw her crack a smile as she looked though it.

I might have to change my mind about Adrian. He's giving 'Daniel' a run for his money.

What does that even mean, 'A run for his money'? Is it a sprint or a marathon? And what cash are we referring to? Maybe Adrian knows.

Song Stuck In My Head: "Boys", by Robots In Disguise

**

Entry #12: 10/15/07, 4:45pm

Today I'm Feeling: victimized

It's so unfair.

I knew it. Mom got home in the middle of the night last night, and she was sobbing so loud that it woke me up. I snuck halfway down the stairs and managed to hear her talking to Aunt T@mmi3 – something like "De\/in turned away from us, so he had to be tracked down." Then she was on the phone with Dad at work, telling him the same thing, and crying over how valuable 'De\/in' had been. Then she and Aunt T@mmi3 went down to the basement and chanted. I listened for twenty minutes or so, but I was tired so I went back to bed.

This morning Mom, Dad and Aunt T@mmi3 are around the breakfast table looking like they're all still awake from last night. I ask them what happened but of course they won't tell me anything. The most I get is Mom saying that she "lost a client." I asked if that meant he was dead, but Mom didn't answer me. She just hugged me tight, crying quietly onto my shoulder for like five minutes. Did that feel weird!

So I give them another hour or so to calm down, then go back to ask Mom about going to the mall with Deni & Mel. She says no, she needs me to stay around the house today. I argued, I wailed, I screamed, but they weren't having it. Even Aunt T@mmi3 shrugged her shoulders at me, as if to say 'nothing I can do can change their insanity'.

I don't get it. What does Mom 'losing a client' have to do with me going to the freaking mall? Nothing, that's what! Are they afraid I'll become hooked on drugs at the MALL?! They're so unreasonable!

Ugh! I swear my parents are determined to keep me from doing anything normal for all of my teenage years. I can NOT wait until I turn 18 and I don't have to answer to them any more. Then maybe I could do fun things, NORMAL things with my life!

In the meantime, I have another Saturday stuck at home. Fantastic!

Song Stuck In My Head: "Why Does It Always Rain On Me", Travis

**

Entry #13: 10/16/07, 11:30pm

Today I'm feeling: like a refugee

We had a drill today.

WEIRD THINGS ABOUT MY FAMILY:

#4) Every now and then my dad will barge into my room and say "Pack your things, DanneR. We have to go." And then I have one minute to grab as much stuff as I can carry and make it downstairs to the garage.

"Hit The Road" drills have been a part of my life for as long as I can remember. At first they were fun – seeing how fast I could pack my most treasured dolls & stuffed animals, then taking a little day trip as dad timed how fast we got out of town. Now I just keep a duffel bag in the closet packed with clothes.

One time we actually did leave a town for good in less than ten minutes. I remember sitting in the backseat, asking why we weren't stopping, and Mom answered that it wasn't safe there any more, that bad people were searching for us and so we had to go. I remember feeling glad – the city we lived in was crowded and had a weird smell, and there were bullies at school and I didn't have any friends to watch out for me. But I was worried about the "bad people."

Mom said they were after us because of our religion, that they hated us and would put us in separate jails where they'd do terrible things to us. So it was very important that when we reached our new home to not tell ANYONE about Z or the chanting we did.

What I think really happened is that one of mom's 'clients' went nuts and started stalking her. Mom's really pretty. Picture mid-90's Madeleine Stowe but with dark reddish-brown hair. Or maybe a client had some connections to the mob or something. Whatever, we moved around a lot anyway, so we just left. We didn't talk to the police because Dad is super-paranoid of cops. He says they have too much power. But that's a different story.

I think the bouncing-around days are behind us. We haven't moved in two years, and both rents say they really like it here, and that as long as we're 'careful' we shouldn't have to move ever again. Whatever that means.

But we still have those drills around once a month. It's freaking weird.

Gotta run. The end of another crappy weekend.

DanneR

Song Stuck In My Head: "Run, Run, Run", Phoenix

**

Entry #14: 10/17/07, 8:42pm

Today I'm Feeling: alonealonealone

Mondays suck.

So Deni tells me I missed out meeting Mel's older brother Corbett on Saturday. Apparently he's really cute and very funny. He goes to the alternative high school – Deni thinks he was a troublemaker. Doesn't really matter. The way my life is going, I'll never meet him.

Melissa got me some socks with Raven on them. (Raven from the Teen Titans cartoon) They're silly. I hope I smile more than Raven does. But these days I know all about having to control your emotions like she does.

Adrian ignored me today. When I asked him if anything was wrong, he just said he had a lot of work to do on his project. I wonder if I missed my opportunity.

Opportunity for what, though? Do I really want him to be my MaleFriend?

HAHAHAHAHAHAHAHAHAHAHAHA

Me have a MaleFriend? Very funny. When would I ever see this supposed MaleFriend? What's the point?

Why does time go so slowly for me? It feels like I've been 15 forever. I wish I could wake up to be 18, leave my parents' place, go do whatever I wanted.

Damn it.

Song Stuck In My Head: "Last", by Gravity Kills

**

Entry #15: 10/18/07, 8:30pm

Today I'm Feeling: crappy

I feel crappy.

I didn't sleep much last night. Just watched adult swim. There's this weird cartoon called Inuyasha, about this time-traveling girl who's friends with all these demons and half-demons. I didn't understand most of it, but I liked that she was friends with these creatures that everybody else would assume are evil.

Adrian didn't say anything to me today. Not one word. But who cares? Not like I could do anything with him if I wanted to.

I don't know why I'm bothering to keep this journal. I haven't heard from most of my online friends in weeks. Where are you, SomNaut? I miss chatting with you...

Only 499 days 'til I turn 18...

DanneR

Song Stuck In My Head: "Summoning of the Muse", by Dead Can Dance

**

Entry #16: 10/19/07, 8:41pm

Today I'm Feeling: somnambulant

One of my more interesting days.

So one minute I'm sitting in Geometry, just kinda staring off into space. I remember a weird smell, and then the next minute I'm lying on top of a bookcase in the library. That's right, on **top** of a ten-foot bookcase. Nobody's around, and when I climb down I find that almost two hours have passed.

Deni asked me where I went instead of going to English. I told her I just walked around the school, dodging the monitors.

I don't really know what to make of this. I think I just fell asleep in class – it wouldn't be the first time. But I've never sleptwalk before, that I know of. Is there such a thing as sleepclimbing? And how come nobody saw me asleep on **top** of the bookcase?

I haven't told the rents or Aunt T@mmi3. I'm not sure why. I think it was just kinda nice to have two hours of the day shoot by like that. Like hitting chapter-skip on the DVD. Let's get this boring crap over with and skip ahead to the good stuff.

Assuming I have any good stuff in my future. Maybe when I turn 18.

What sucks about all this is that my chances for getting any sleep tonight are worse than normal, what with my little walking nap earlier in the day. Oh well. Maybe Inuyasha will be on again and I can get more of an idea of what the hell is going on.

DanneR

Song Stuck In My Head: "Sleepwalking", by Blindside

**

Entry #17: 10/21/07, 6:45pm

Today I'm Feeling: frightened

Weird stuff. Weird, scary stuff.

I stayed home from school, and the house is filled with aunts and uncles. They're all here because of yesterday.

All I remember is that I was working on my painting, and then I woke up on the floor in a girls bathroom on the other side of the school. It was two hours later, and my hands were covered in something sticky.

It didn't take me long to figure out that the stuff on my hands was dried blood. But I don't know whose. I didn't have any marks on me, though.

I scrubbed it off and called Aunt T@mmi3, who sent Uncle V to come get me. He kept asking me if I remembered feeling pissed off before it happened. But I don't remember feeling anything, at least nothing I haven't felt every day of high school. Strange, bored, alone...

I told my story to my parents and Aunt T@mmi3, including what happened the day before, with the waking up on the bookshelf, and then their faces got real serious. They said I should have told them about that right after it happened, that I should tell them whenever anything weird happens to me. They sent me to my room and told me to get some sleep.

How did that blood get on my hands? Whose was it? What did I do?

I called Deni, trying to be vague about why I wanted to know if the cops had been to the school yesterday. She said not that she knew of.

Maybe it was my own blood. Maybe I had a nosebleed and somehow washed my face without using my hands. Yeah, right.

I snuck downstairs to try to listen to the rents, but they found me and hustled me back upstairs. Then they parked Uncle V in the hallway so I couldn't leave.

Eventually Aunt T@mmi3 came to my room and said she thinks I'm having withdrawal from the Last Resort, that it's messing with my sleep pattern. So what do we do about it?

She said I need to detox my system, and that's done with something called a "Cleansing." That's why all the aunts and uncles are here. They're going to perform some ritual of Z over me in the basement. Aunt T@mmi3 said it's going to hurt a little, but when it's all over I'll feel refreshed. Not like the Last Resort, though.

This "Cleansing" happens tomorrow. I'm nervous about it, but more nervous about what I might have done to get that blood on my hands. The rents don't want me telling anybody what happened, but I have to ask Deni if she knows anything. How else am I going to find out?

I gotta run. Right now I'm more scared of myself than I've ever been of any 'bad people.'

Song Stuck In My Head: "Am I Demon", by Danzig

**

Entry #18: 10/23/07, 11:17pm

Today I'm Feeling: aflame

The past two days have been a nightmare of pain. Everything hurts, especially my head and this place just beneath my heart where the pain seems somehow more concentrated. I've only just become able to string some coherent thoughts together, so I thought I'd better write while I could.

The Cleansing happened in the basement two nights ago. My parents were there, and most of my 'aunts' and 'uncles' – Aunt T@mmi3, Uncle V, Auntie Nikki, Unkie Louie, Aunt Josie – all sitting a circle. They had me lie down on the concrete in the middle, and then they started chanting. I couldn't understand what they were saying - I think it was in Greek or Romanian or something – but it was really hypnotic and I started to feel warm and sleepy. They told me to expect that, so I closed my eyes.

This is where it gets all fuzzy. I remember feeling weightless, like I was floating up to the ceiling, and I heard this deep voice call my name.

And then pain.

It was like two explosions – one in my brain and one in that place just beneath my heart, and my veins carried liquid fire all throughout me. And it wouldn't stop. The pain just kept spreading and building. I screamed, I tried to thrash around but I felt hands holding my shins and elbows down. And the pain kept on burning through me.

I remember thinking 'I am the h0urg1a55, and the flames are going to crack me. All my sand will spill onto the floor and I will be no more.' Eventually I passed out.

I woke up in my bed around 8 hours later, and it felt like my brain and heart were sore. It hurt to breathe, and I was really achy and nauseous. Aunt T@mmi3 was there, and she asked me if I needed to puke. I said I didn't, but I was wrong. I got most of it into the bucket. She had me drink a glass of water, and then I had another 5 hours of dreams where I'm on fire and my parents are holding me down so the flames can reach every inch of skin on my body.

Aunt T@mmi3 said the Cleansing went well. When I asked her about the pain, she said that was the trade-off for all the good it was doing inside me. I figure they spiked my dinner with some drug and then just chanted at me until it started doing its thing. It's just like my mother to turn all this into religious drama.

I wonder what was really done to me...

I'm still worried about what I did at school to end up with blood on my hands, but my parents say we're going to find out tomorrow. I'll write again when I know more.

DanneR

Song Stuck In My Head: "Your Ex-Lover Is Dead", by Stars

**

Entry #19: 10/24/07, 7:20pm

Today I'm Feeling: nervous

Another day home from school. I'm feeling better – not as energized as when I was on the Last Resort, but a bit more like the me I knew before I got sick. I guess that's a good thing.

Uncle V took some blood from me today. When we were finished he put the vial in a lockbox, which he then handcuffed to his wrist. Who would possibly be interested in my blood? He's such a weirdo. He's way older than my parents and he's got these creepy eyes that float in the whites like blue beach balls bobbing in an ocean of milk. But my parents trust him, and Aunt T@mmi3 gets a faraway smile on her face whenever she talks about him.

Anyway, after he took the blood he hypnotized me to see if we could dig up any memories of how I got that blood on my hands. It was weird, one second I'm staring at this candle flame, and then I hear Uncle V's fingers snap, and the candle is an inch lower.

So what happened in that time I can't remember?

Apparently Adrian got a nosebleed, a real bad one. I got him some tissue and held it to his face, which was where all the blood came from. I went with him to the door of the boys' bathroom. Then – after Adrian had gone inside without me – the sight and smell of all that blood on the tissues was too much for me and I felt faint. I went into the girls' bathroom and passed out.

Combine all that with the withdrawal from the Last Resort, and I guess it makes sense... The smell of blood has always made me nauseous. And like Mom, I freak out at the sight. I must really like Adrian if I was able to overcome those feelings until he was away.

But then why was I in the bathroom across the school? And what happened the day before, when I ended up on top of that bookshelf?

Uncle V said we'd look into the bookshelf 'another time' but he didn't seem worried. And it looks like I'm going to be healthy enough to go to school tomorrow. The rents seem pretty sure that the 'Cleansing' will prevent any more blackouts.

I don't want to go. I'd like another few days of not blacking out, but the rents are convinced. I think I'll get Deni and Mel to help me out with this...

DanneR

Song Stuck In My Head: "Hypnotized", by Paul Oakenfold

**

Entry #20: 10/25/07, 8:44pm

Today I'm Feeling: like a pincushion

A relatively normal day at school, for a change. I'm exhausted from trying to stay awake. To make sure, I asked Deni & Mel to pinch me if I look like I'm sleepwalking. I didn't give anything away, just told them I keep getting in trouble by falling asleep in class, which isn't a lie.

So right away they start pinching me every five minutes. Ha Ha.

Adrian was there, and he asked how I was. He said I looked really sick last week, that I was flushed and sweating. Sweet of him to ask. I asked him to pinch me if I looked like I was nodding off, and he smiled and said "Who am I to take you away from a dream?"

When I got home the rents grilled me on how my day went. They looked really relieved when I told them everything was cool. They even liked my plan to have Deni & Mel pinch me.

All my aunts and uncles are gone, except Aunt T@mmi3. She said Uncle V will have the results of my bloodwork tomorrow, but she thinks I'm "out of the woods." But I like the woods. It's nice and shady there.

DanneR

Song Stuck In My Head: "Tell Me About the Forest (You Once Called Home)", by Dead Can Dance

**

Entry #21: 10/26/07, 7:20pm

Today I'm Feeling: annoyed

Way too many boys in my life right now.

Boy 1: Adrian. Saw him chatting with Tiff Warnock this morning. She's a cheerleader with mascara for brains. I mentioned my opinion of her during Painting, and he defended her, saying she was actually a very sweet person.

Oops.

How can he like someone so vacant? She thinks about nothing but makeup and pep rallies. If he likes her, I must not know Adrian very well at all. That happens to me with boys. I get to thinking I know one, and then it turns out he's actually an a$$hole. I've never been really sure one way or the other with Adrian.

Boy 2: Clint. He's this really creepy guy with greasy hair who always wears a trenchcoat and smells like baby-wipes. He was pestering me at lunch today. He kept calling me 'Jill' and asking me where my pail of water was. Mel threw French fries at him, chasing him off by yelling "Pi$$ off, you Klebold wannabe!" I wish I had Mel's guts.

Boy 3: Tigerbug Guy. I don't know his name, but he stopped by the main entrance while I was waiting for Aunt T@mmi3 to pick me up. He was driving a bright orange VW bug with black Bengal-tiger stripes decaled all over it. He comes right up to me and asks if I need a ride. I said "apparently."

He says "let's go, then."

I say my ride is already coming, and that I don't know him from Adam.

He's all "who's Adam? Is he your boyfriend? Do you think I could take him? Or is he a football player or something?"

And he grins. "Nah, you don't look like the type to be into jocks."

And he won't leave me alone. I had to endure ten more minutes of his cutesy flirting until Aunt T@mmi3 finally rescued me.

It goes like this for me. Months of no boys, then way too much of them. I wish they would spread it out a little.

I gotta go, but Aunt T@mmi3 told me my blood 'looked good', and she thinks this whole sick and sleepwalking stuff is over. I guess we'll see. I still wonder about that first day, waking up on top of the bookcase, but Uncle V left town today, and I don't know when he'll be back. In the meantime I'm trying not to think about it.

DanneR

Song Stuck In My Head: "Leave Me Alone", by Killing Heidi

**

Entry #22: 10/27/07, 6:40pm

Today I'm Feeling: icky

I got this note in my locker today:

Jill,

Ill give u $5 if u let me no wen ur next performince is. Ill even cum on stage wit u if u want.

Jack (Lockr 214)

It's Clint again. What a creep! Deni says he just wants my attention, which he's not gonna get. I don't even want to know what he's rambling about. He's grosser than gross.

Mom and Aunt T@mmi3 were arguing tonight. I'd never heard Aunt T@mmi3 raise her voice before. They were in my rents' room and I couldn't make out much, but Aunt T@mmi3 said something like "We're always on new ground! I'm sorry that I'm not perfect!"

Mom ended up apologizing and I could hear her crying. I think she misses Dad. He's been working a lot (some kind of flood upriver, or something), and it seems like his days off always match up with Mom's out of town trips. She always acts different with him around. Way more mellow, unless she's lost a client.

Sometimes I hear her on the phone with him really late at night. Each time I hear her she says "I hate being apart from you. It's like I'm missing part of myself, and nothing I can do can fill that void in my heart."

I wonder if I'll get all melodramatic when I get married. Assuming I ever find a man. I hope I don't get all co-dependent. But if I did, I guess that would mean I really loved somebody. Would that really be so bad?

Tomorrow is Friday, hurrah. My last three weekends have all sucked, so it doesn't mean much to me anymore.

DanneR

Song Stuck In My Head: "Fade Into You", by Mazzy Star

**

Entry #23: 10/28/07, 6:30pm

Today I'm Feeling: hurt

Weird Friday. First Clint came up to my locker, all hooting and making rude gestures with his fingers. I got so mad that I punched his arm, but he just laughed. I should tell a teacher or something, but the less my teachers notice me when I'm there, the less they'll notice when I'm gone. And I tend to be gone a lot.

Then, when I'm bitching about Clint in Painting, Adrian starts saying what a cute couple Clint and I would be! It was obvious how much I hate Clint, but Adrian kept it up. I think he was trying to be funny, but I just got so frustrated. I almost cried. I could feel the tears in my eyes, but I kept him from seeing. I wanted sympathy, and he gave me ridicule, and for some reason that really, really hurt today.

Mel wants Deni & me to hang out at the coast with her & Corbett this weekend, and I said I'd try, but I don't like my chances. Aunt T@mmi3 is out of town, so it's just me and the rents this weekend. Maybe I'll get lucky.

Ew, not like that! Get your mind out of the gutter.

Then again, who am I talking to?

DanneR

Song Stuck In My Head: "Burden In My Hand," Soundgarden

**

Entry #24: 10/29/07, 9:30pm

Today I'm Feeling: Tired & Happy

Realization: Corbett (Mel's brother) = Tigerbug Guy.

By some miracle, my parents let me go with Deni, Mel and Corbett to the coast. I think the rents just wanted some time together, and their 'needs' overcame their paranoia about me for a day.

GROSS.

But if that's what it takes, then I'm not going to complain. I'm just not going to think about it.

Anyway, turns out it was Corbett who was being so flirty with me on Thursday. Deni was right, he is kind of cute. He's got really big eyes that are always wide and darting, like he's always thinking of some trick to pull. He wears a gray fedora all the time, and a red tie with the knot hung down low.

He's a big goofball! He asked me how Adam was, and Mel says no, my Internet boyfriend's name is Daniel, and so I say that things with "Daniel" and I had been over for more than a week, and I could tell that Corbett knew I was totally making up the whole Daniel thing, but he played along.

Anyway, we spent the day throwing the Frisbee along the beaches and generally acting weird around what Corbett calls "the straights," especially those girls that wear a ton of makeup and do their hair really fancy to *go to the beach.* Corbett kept shouting "GO BACK TO THE DOCKS!" from the window of the Tigerbug before speeding away as Deni, Mel and I shrieked with laughter.

He really gets along with Mel, which I've never seen with brothers and sisters. Mel says he's got great taste in music. The stuff he played in the Tigerbug was a little too punkish for me, but it definitely wasn't the crap I hear on the radio.

So now I'm home, and I'm exhausted, and I know I got sunburnt something awful, but it was a great time!

The rents seem happy too. Mom was sitting on Dad's lap when I got home, giggling. Mom's not the giggling type, so they must've had a good day. So we all did!

DanneR

Song Stuck In My Head: "Today", Smashing Pumpkins

**

Entry #25: 10/30/07, 9:33am

Today I'm Feeling: crispy

Yep, I'm burnt.

Apparently I missed applying the sunblock to my neck entirely, because it's really raw today. My nose is bright pink. Dad says I look like I tried to stir-fry my face.

Mom gave me some cream, and she doesn't think it's bad enough to get Aunt T@mmi3. Mom is very sun sensitive. She says it makes her itch. She's always happy when it's rainy out, because then she can run errands and go shopping all day.

Sunburns have always made me sleepy, so I think I'll just lounge on the couch with dad as he watches football all day. The sound of the game usually puts me right out.

DanneR

Song Stuck in My Head: "Catch the Sun", by Doves

**

Entry #26: 10/31/07, 7:30pm

questions

I don't know what it means. I don't know what to believe.

I had to go to the library today for my history class. It was the first time I'd gone since the sleepclimbing. Clint was there and he immediately comes to my table and starts whispering about "is Jill back for another show." I kinda lost it and yelled at him. Why does he keep bugging me? What did I ever do to him?

Then he got all serious. He said he admires my guts, that he'd thought about doing what I did, but could never get up the courage.

When I asked him what the hell he was talking about, he pointed across the way, to that corner of the library, where I woke up last week.

I got this hot feeling just below my heart. I asked Clint what he thought I was doing up there.

He looked me in the eye, smiled, and said, "I think it's pretty obvious what you were doing up there, *Jill*."

Clint saw me. But I still don't remember anything about it.

Every time I look at that shelf my heart starts pounding and I get short of breath. Why won't Clint just tell me what he saw? Maybe he knows I won't believe him. And why is he calling me Jill?

More importantly, why am I paying any attention to this freak? I guess it's because he's the only one who can really tell me what I was doing during those times that I can't remember.

But I don't know what to do now.

DanneR

Song Stuck In My Head: "In Limbo," Radiohead

**

Entry #27: 11/1/07, 5:45am

Oh my god.

http://www.urbandictionary.com/define.php?term=jack+and+jill

Is *that* what I was doing up on that shelf? Clint obviously thinks so.

Why does he think that? Is he just a delusional creep? Or was I really…

I've got to find out, but I don't know how.

What kind of person does that stuff in a public place?

Am I that kind of person?

**

Entry #28: 11/1/07, 11:03pm

confused

I'm in a daze. Everything's out of focus, and people's voices are flat. It's like I'm haunting my own body.

Another shock today in Painting. I was sitting there, thinking about that website I found last night, and Adrian nudges me. He says I look really intense, like after he came out of the bathroom when he had that bloody nose. Like I was trying to crack a safe, or hear the termites in the walls.

I say no, I didn't see you when you came out. I went into the girl's room.

He says no, you were standing right there, with that same look on your face. He says I told him that I felt queasy but that I wanted to make sure he felt okay. He says I said I'd be back in just a minute, but then he never saw me again.

This does not jive with what Uncle V told me I said under hypnosis.

? What the hell? Adrian has no reason to lie to me about a little detail like that.

So that means Uncle V lied to me about what I said under hypnosis. I know he recorded our conversation, and this evening I asked Mom if I could hear the tape.

She said Uncle V has it, but I really shouldn't worry about the past. There's nothing anyone can do to change it, she said.

She didn't change her attitude when I told her that some details aren't matching. She said Adrian must be mistaken, or I'm remembering wrong. That happens with memories, she says. In any case, I should forget about it and move on.

I didn't tell her about Clint.

I know I'm never getting my hands on that tape. And even if I could track down Uncle V, I bet he would sing the same song that Mom did.

Are they really lying to me? Why would they do that? More so-called 'protecting' me from the world?

Or maybe I did something awful and my parents are just trying to cover it up.

I've got to find out what really happened during those two days at school. I've got to know what I'm capable of. But how?

Maybe I'll remember something if I return to the scenes. I haven't been back to that girl's room on the other side of the school yet. And I haven't seen that library shelf up close.

I'll do it tomorrow.

**

Entry #29: 11/2/07, 6:45 pm

More bits. More questions.

I poked around that girl's restroom. When I was in the stall where I woke up, I had a new memory: flushing the toilet over and over again. But when I try to think about why I was flushing, like what was in the bowl, it gets really fuzzy. And that place below my heart throbs like a hammered finger.

I went into the library – lucky for me Clint wasn't there – and I went to that shelf. My heart pounds, and I start breathing heavily, and when I touch the shelf, I get a vision:

A boy with dark hair, older than me but still high school age, holding a red cloth to his eyebrow. Blood is spilling down his cheek, down his neck in little streams. The eyebrow is swelling, and he's got a swollen lower lip. I didn't recognize the face.

I saw the vision, and that place below my heart throbbed like a stubbed toe.

I spent a couple hours going through my old yearbooks, but I didn't see that face. So who the hell is that boy? And did he really inspire me to sneak to the library, climb a ten-foot bookshelf and start Jilling up there?

That's CRAZY! I would never, ever do that in public! All my experimenting - and believe me, it's been tame and infrequent - has been done at home, behind locked doors.

Maybe it's not as innocent as that. Maybe I hurt that boy, and couldn't contain the ecstasy I felt from the act.

Maybe I killed him and stashed the body somewhere. Then climbed that shelf to celebrate.

No, that's even CRAZIER! I could never do that, not even to Clint!

But the fact remains that I don't know what I did on either of those days, and my parents don't **want** me to know.

I wish I had somebody to talk to about this. I'm afraid I'm spiraling, digging down deeper from delusion to delusion, and nobody's at the surface to throw down a rope.

Talking to the ether is comforting, but the ether doesn't provide many answers. Just nonjudgmental silence.

...I just thought of someone I could ask. I should've put it together when that place below my heart kept hurting.

I can try to talk to Z. *(see weird thing #2)*

Not that I really believe in Z. But there's some connection between my memories and that feeling I got from the Cleansing, so maybe something will come to mind if I meditate down there.

I don't know what else to do.

...Crap, Mom's down there chanting. It could be hours. I'll have to try tomorrow.

DanneR

**

Entry #30: 11/3/07, 6:32pm

waiting

Mom is tired. I bet she's going to bed soon, and then I'll have my chance.

School took forever, and I think I was really bitchy to my friends. I told them my parents were fighting. At least I know one thing about myself: I'm a liar.

But really, what would I say? "There's parts of two days that I don't remember, but at the end of one I had blood all over my hands and at the end of the other it looks like I was masturbating on top of a bookshelf. So I'm a little on edge."

I just heard Mom's door close. Now's my chance.

**

Entry #31: 11/3/07, 10:19pm

the difference between nightmare and memory

What I just had was both.

I chanted for a while ('I want to remember') and then my mind wandered. I had visions of what happened in that time that I can't remember.

I did some freakish things. Disturbing, perverted things. The visions connect the dots, but in such a messed-up way that I get really scared just thinking about it. No way am I typing them here.

Maybe those visions were just my imagination. But I have a way to check. I saw things at the school in the vision, parts of the school I've never seen before. I've got details branded into my memory.

I'll go to school tomorrow, and those details won't be there, and I'll just chalk it up to a bad trip or something. And I'll never go down to the basement again.

**

Entry #32: 11/4/07, 6:44pm

epiphany

It's all true. The visions showed me what I really did, and ~~who~~ what I really am.

I snuck into the boys room, and the initials MLG were carved into the wall above the trash can. I moved the ceiling tile in that empty classroom and saw the orange spray-painted P.

I have new respect for Z. And new contempt for myself.

I'm a freak. I'm a monster. I should be locked up before I kill someone.

How many other times have I done this kind of freaky thing?

I can't escape the feeling that this is who I really am. Beneath my boring, ordinary surface is the real freakish me. A pervert.

Clint and I really would make a good couple.

That last thought alone makes me want to scream until my lungs explode.

**

Entry #33: 11/5/07, 8:58pm

and then they will dissolve

My glass has cracked, and my black sands have spilled out before me.

It wasn't the sexual nature of the episodes. Everybody has the hormones and the parts for that.

It was the blood. It *is* the blood. The bleeding cut over that boy's eyebrow. Adrian's bloody tissues all over my hands. They set me off.

They revealed my true nature. One that delights in the pain of others.

I am standing at the bottom of a well, and the rain is slowly pushing the water level past my knees. I'm holding my black sands above my head. But they will be mud soon. And then they will dissolve.

And still my parents do nothing. Maybe they're fooling themselves, pretending it's just a phase, that it'll go away like a fad. Like when I wanted to be a tap-dancer when I was nine.

Or maybe they do know, they've always known. I'm the reason we don't see regular doctors, why we've moved so much. They're just waiting for the one destructive act to put me away forever. After all, I haven't really hurt anyone yet.

Eaten a trashcan's worth of bloody tissue, yes.

Touched myself on top of a bookcase in the school library, yes.

But hurt someone, no.

Maybe I need to hurt myself to get their attention.

I wonder if I have the courage for that.

**

Entry #34: 11/6/07, 4:02pm

the most wonderful thing that's ever happened

I can't sleep. I keep having dreams like this:

I run inside our house from being out in the sun, and I feel like I need a shower and I turn on the faucet and I step under the streams and it's all over me and I'm really excited and I wash my hair with it and my knees are weak and I'm squirming in a puddle of thick filmy blood and it's the most wonderful thing that's ever happened.

Can vampires survive in the daylight? Everything I've read says they can't. Except 'Blade', but he was only half. And he was a muscular black man. I'm a skinny white chick. Besides, I know that vampires don't exist.

Psychopaths do, though.

I am rudderless at sea, just drifting where the waves will take me. With my black sands cupped in my hands.

If I made coffee from my sand, how would the drink taste? Like cyanide? Sour milk? Flat cola?

If I made Adrian drink the coffee from my black sands, what would happen?

Would he become like me? Thrilled to see someone's life spilling onto his hands?

Or would he puke his guts out, set fire to his tongue and scrape the enamel off his teeth?

Or would he start to bleed?

**

Entry #35: 11/6/07, 11:58pm

siren

I just screamed at my parents for a while, saying I remembered the blacked-out time and that I'm going crazy and I should be committed. They said I was being irrational, but if I insisted, they'd have me talk to a therapist. I said fine.

When I convince this shrink that I'm crazy they'll have to put me away. I don't get to see him until Wednesday. I hope I don't hurt my friends before then.

Yes, they're making me go to school. They said being around other people will take my mind off things.

It's on their heads if I freak out and hurt someone.

Who am I kidding. Of course it's on my own head. I'm the one living in this body. I just need to keep control of myself.

**

Entry #36: 11/7/07, 8:50pm

there's nothing to be done

I'm walking on a balance beam. Below me is a fall so great that I can't see the bottom. And a fierce wind is blowing.

I kept crying at school today, which seemed to distract both the other kids and my teachers. Everybody kept asking me if I wanted to talk about it. I always answered with "There's nothing to be done."

I didn't do anything bizarre or hurt any friends. Though I nearly decked Deni in English. It took me half a second to remember that I'd asked her to pinch me whenever I looked like I was drifting to sleep. I wonder what I would have done if she *hadn't* pinched me.

This beam I'm walking down, I'm not sure where it's going. It might end in a big pot of boiling oil for all I know. I've got to keep my eyes on my feet, because I know I don't want to fall.

Corbett found me waiting outside again. But he wasn't cutesy. Maybe Mel told him how weird I've been acting. He didn't ask me if I wanted to talk about it. He just sat next to me on the sidewalk and offered me his headphones.

This incredible song was playing. It didn't have any singing, but it still sounded so wonderfully, stunningly sad...

Before I knew it I was asking Corbett if he'd ever done anything that he'd never thought he was truly capable of doing.

He nodded. Then he lit a cigarette and said,

"Finding out what you're truly capable of makes every good thing you do that much more meaningful. It makes every moment that you resist temptation a significant victory, because you know exactly what you can do if you ever relent.

"But if you've got a decent soul, that bad thing, that mistake you made that led to your self-discovery, it'll haunt you. And it doesn't seem to ever go away."

He didn't tell me what he'd done, and he didn't ask what I'd done. He just gave me his cell number and told me I could call him if I ever wanted to talk.

It was just 5 minutes, but it was like the wind stopped blowing and that balance beam became a sidewalk. For a while, anyway.

I don't think I can call him, though. I might accidentally tell him the freakish things I did. And then he'd never want to speak to me again.

That makes me sadder than I've ever felt before.

Song Forever Stuck In My Head: "Fragments of Memories", Yasunori Mitsuda

**

Entry #37 : 11/8/07, 6:45pm

revelations

Wow, where to begin? I guess with school, which was another struggle to stay awake and not get paralyzed with fear whenever anyone mentioned the future. I really hoped Corbett would show again, but no luck.

When Mom and I get to the house, Dad's awake, and Aunt T@mmi3 and Uncle V are there. "DanneR," Dad said, "it's time you knew the truth."

Yes, they'd heard everything on the tape, but they don't think I did any of it. I tell them that I know I did, I remember things like those initials in the boys bathroom, that spray- painted P in the ceiling.

But my dad said he remembered the P from the open house last year. That room was where my Geography teacher was, and the ceiling tile was moved for some kind of maintenance, and he'd seen that P and made a bad joke about if this is the P room, he sure didn't want to see what was in the BM room.

And one day Uncle V picked me up from school because I was sick; he used the boy's bathroom, then asked me if I knew anybody with the initials MLG, because he liked their work. Somehow MLG had managed to carve his (her?) initials into solid concrete.

So I'd never seen the P or the MLG, but I'd been told about both of them.

So I was confused, but Aunt T@mmi3 started to explain. The Last Resort contains a powerful – and illegal – hallucinogen called UNR34; and on those two days I was a little sleep-deprived, and that was enough to get me to do some tripping. In that hypnosis session with Uncle V I reported what I'd hallucinated. I later remembered it during that chanting in the basement.

Apparently people are mostly zombies while they're tripping on UNR34, and that's probably all I did during the trip: just kinda space out and drool a little. We'll never know why I decided to climb that shelf in the library, but Aunt T@mmi3 thinks it was because I was cold, and I thought it might be warmer up there. She thinks Clint didn't see me touching myself. I was shivering and rubbing my skin to get warm.

This UNR34 dredges up stuff from the darkest parts of your subconscious and practically brings that stuff to life. In my case I saw myself doing these wild, bizarre things that a cavewoman might do. My family didn't tell me because if I didn't remember what I hallucinated, then I wouldn't be disturbed by how strange I **thought** I was acting. They just wanted to get me to move on; they didn't count on me remembering it on my own.

So why the hell was I given a powerful hallucinogen?

Because I've needed the UNR34 all my life. It's the best treatment they've found for my illness.

Apparently I have an extremely rare disorder in my blood, something about white blood cells being unpredictably aggressive toward regular stuff in my body. The doctors in a major city in the eastern United States that rhymes with 'Floston' knew that UNR34, besides making people trip profoundly, happened to do a decent job on getting my whiteys to behave. But the doctors didn't see regular doses of UNR34 as an acceptable treatment – they said they didn't want me to spend my life tripping off and on. So they convinced my parents to let them try some experimental drugs on me.

And I nearly died in the process. Spent three weeks in a coma when I was 2.

This apparently made my already distrustful parents swear off doctors forever. But the only drug they knew that could help me was a controlled substance.

So they stole a crapload from a pharmacy and left town.

They've been managing my dosage of UNR34 with Aunt T@mmi3's help all my life. Apparently Aunt T@mmi3 is brilliant, because I don't need much anymore. And while I used to trip a lot as a kid, I'd just zombie out for a while and I never remembered what I saw when I tripped. This latest episode happened because Aunt T@mmi3's dose of UNR34 was a little too strong.

She apologized over and over to me, said she'd give me some sleep-aids that I'll take for two weeks after my next dose of The Last Resort, and that should hopefully keep me from tripping.

Well, this certainly explains the doctor thing.

Apparently UNR34 will show up in any urine or blood sample I give because my body is teeming with it. To anybody looking in it looks like my parents are feeding me acid pretty regularly. And it explains why Dad has always been dodgy about police. For all he knows, he and mom are still wanted in a major eastern city that rhymes with 'Floston.'

What I don't get is the secrecy. Why not just tell me so I could be prepared for any tripping?

They said they wanted me to live as normal a life as possible, to at least think that I was just like everybody else. I guess I can understand that.

My brain is swimming with thoughts, but I gotta go. I guess the most important thing is that it looks like I didn't actually do those freaky things. But I'm dependent on a controlled substance, and it looks like I will be for the rest of my life.

DanneR

**

Entry #38: 11/9/07, 9:20pm

better!

Wow, do I feel better. It's like that balance beam has been replaced by a wide, rolling prairie and the winds are calm.

I apologized to Deni & Mel for acting so strangely. They were cool about it – "we all have our rough patches" – but they wish I'd share with them what was going on. Real friends tell each other things. I told them that I had a bad reaction to some 'behavioral medicine', and implied that my parents were fighting.

I wonder if I'll ever stop lying. But I can't just tell my friends that I'm dependent on an illegal/illicit drug and will be for the rest of my life. Not that they'd rat me or my parents out. I just don't think they'd believe me. And I'd rather actually be a liar than be thought one.

I didn't see Corbett today, but he's got a hug coming his way when I do. One of these days I'll get up the courage to call him.

So I'm on this UNR34 for the rest of my life. But it won't be so bad. I only need it every once in a while now, and Aunt T@mmi3 will show me how she makes her mixtures. She says she's got enough of it to last me about 50 years.

I can never go to a doctor, but I've got Aunt T@mmi3, and when she gets too old she'll pass on her knowledge to another friend of the family. I can't have kids, of course, but I knew that already.

I do wonder what having all that UNR34 in my system for so many years has done to me, though. Maybe it's where my paintings come from. And maybe my dreams are all memories of the trips I've taken.

Who knows?

I wish my parents would trust me a little more, stop trying to protect me from everything. If they'd just told me the truth I wouldn't have gone through all this. Maybe this episode has taught them something.

But I doubt it.

DanneR

Song Stuck In My Head: "Trust", Megadeth

**

Entry #39: 11/12/07, 3:45 pm

Hello DanneR Partiers,

This is Uncle PJ, the web guy. I just wanted to let all of you know that I got word today that DanneR and her family had to suddenly move from their prior location. I don't know the details, but I will be meeting up with them later on this week. I will let you know then if DanneR is planning to continue her blog.

Thanks for reading,

Uncle PJ

**

Entry #40: 11/15/07, 8:19pm

Hello again DanneR Party,

If anyone has heard from DanneR I ask that you please, PLEASE let me know. Her family did not show at our arranged rendezvous, and all prior phone numbers have been changed.

I'm very worried. DanneR has a condition that can be dangerous both to herself and to anyone around her. I can help her, but only if I know where she is. I can be reached at 604-678-5811.

Thanks for your help,

Uncle PJ

PS If you see DanneR InRealLife do *NOT* approach her. Call or Email me immediately with last known whereabouts and I will make sure she is taken care of.

**

Entry #41: 11/17/07, 12:12pm

lost

I don't know where I am. The ground is rocky and dry, and brown mountains line the horizon. I can't see any houses or roads or fences or any other sign of civilization. We've spent two days in this trailer, waiting for what dad calls our 'contact' to get us to some place called 'Bascomville.' There's a gas generator here and a dozen tanks filled with fuel. Countless bottles of water and canned food. Like a bomb shelter whose only real protection is being in the middle of nowhere.

We've been traveling at night, but I keep falling asleep. Each time I wake up it feels a little warmer outside, so we must be going south.

Every time I close my eyes I hope that sleep will somehow spring me from this nightmare.

Something is terribly wrong with mom. I saw the changes happen right in front of me. I keep seeing that red in her eyes, like ripe cherries. It keeps showing up in my reflection.

But I must've imagined it. There's no way all this can be real.

My parents must be lying to me. Probably because they think I can't handle the truth.

Mom's been awake about four hours in the last week. She tells me not to worry, that Z will protect us. But how can you get protection from yourself?

I have to go. If dad wakes up to find me using his laptop and SATphone he'll change all his passwords again.

**

Entry #42: 11/19/07, 7:10pm

Hello Partiers,

I received an email from DanneR today:

Uncle PJ,

Thanks for your concern, and for all your help with my blog. I've moved again. I'm now 1000 miles away from my old life, both from the house I called home, and from the girl I called DanneR.

My parents finally told me the truth, but only because I saw something that unraveled all the lies. Reading my blog shows me where I got my lying techniques. UNR34? What a whopper that was. The thing about my parents' lies is that each one contains 90% truth.

I – and they – really are addicted to something, it just isn't a hallucinogenic drug. I can't believe I didn't figure it out myself.

Of course there aren't many windows in our houses.
Of course they don't go out in the sun much.
Of course Dad had a night job.
Of course Mom loves rainy days.
Of course we've never been to a real doctor or hospital.
Of course I've never come near a church of any kind.
Of course we've moved so many times.

We're addicted to something a lot more common than UNR34, but a whole lot worse. It was in my visions, and now I know it was in the Last Resort.

It's blood. Living, human blood.

My parents are infected with the vampire curse, but Z keeps their symptoms in check. They don't hurt people. They're not evil. Unless you count all the lying. But then that would make me evil too. Maybe I am.

What devastates me the most about all this is that Mom and Dad were infected before I was conceived. They *knew* I'd be cursed from the start, but they let me be born anyway. My 'infection' isn't nearly as bad as theirs, but they still damned me before I took my first breath. Why would they do such a thing?

Maybe they really *are* evil.

Anyway, I'm guessing that if you know my parents, then you knew the truth about us. I know you never lied to me, and I also know that you never told me the truth. But I'm not mad at you. I suspect my parents would've 'punished' you if you told me anything before they did.

I won't be continuing the blog. That DanneR is long gone, and her words were written from behind so many veils of lies that it's pointless to continue. Maybe someday I'll start another blog. But it won't be soon.

I do have a favor to ask, though. Please tell my friends Deni, Mel and Corbett that I'm all right, that my parents are in trouble with the law and that I'll try to visit them someday. I miss the crew, but they can't ever know where I am or why I left. It would mean a lot to me if you did this.

Now I've got to go. I can't promise that I'll stay in touch. I've got a lot to think about these days.

Renna

**

Entry #43: 11/20/07, 10:03pm

It looks like DanneR (real name Warrenna Dennison) won't be posting anymore to this blog. But if you'd like to follow her life, check out

http://patrickvaughn.net

and you may find what you're looking for.

See you on the other side.

Uncle PJ

About the Author

THE STORIES IN THIS COLLECTION FALL INTO THE "contemporary fantasy" category, but most often Patrick Vaughn writes tales containing vampires. They're the most human monster out there, possessing infinite potential to teach us about ourselves. Vampires are smart, charming, scary and sexy, and can manipulate human emotion and passion for their own fiendish benefit. If there's a more terrifying creature of legend, Patrick has not found it.

Patrick has written two young adult novels, "The Cure for the Curse", which won the 2007 Arizona Book Publisher Association's Book of the Year award in the Young Adult category, and its sequel "The Allure of the Curse." The third book in the series, "The Spiral of the Curse," is currently in production. More details can be found at http://patrickvaughn.net.

Patrick lives in El Mirage, Arizona with his wife Misty, with whom he's completely and totally in love.

Made in the USA
San Bernardino, CA
04 September 2013